AF597815

Legend,Gottheil, Richard James Horatio

A selection from the Syriac Julian Romance

Legend,Gottheil, Richard James Horatio

A selection from the Syriac Julian Romance

Inktank publishing, 2018

www.inktank-publishing.com

ISBN/EAN: 9783747797716

All rights reserved

This is a reprint of a historical out of copyright text that has been re-manufactured for better reading and printing by our unique software. Inktank publishing retains all rights of this specific copy which is marked with an invisible watermark.

SEMITIC STUDY SERIES

EDITED BY

RICHARD J. H. GOTTHEIL and MORRIS JASTROW Jr.
Columbia University. University of Pennsylvania,

N⁰. VII.

A SELECTION FROM THE SYRIAC JULIAN ROMANCE

EDITED

WITH A COMPLETE GLOSSARY IN ENGLISH AND GERMAN

BY

RICHARD J. H. GOTTHEIL PH. D.
Prof. of Semitic Languages in Columbia University New-York.

LEIDEN
LATE E. J. BRILL.
1906.

To be had in the U. S. of G. E. Stechert & Co, 129 West 20th Street
New York.

PREFACE.

I have selected for the first Syriac number of the "Semitic Study Series" a portion of the Julian Romance as published by GEORG HOFFMANN [1]); not because of any peculiar interest that attaches to its subject-matter, but because of the excellent Syriac in which it is written, and the freedom of it's language from the influence of Greek constructions. It is an original work, and probably was composed — as NÖLDEKE has shown in a learned essay [2]) — in Edessa and at the beginning of the sixth century. The text, though preserved in only one manuscript for the greater part of the sixth and seventh centuries [3]), has come down to us only moderately deteriorated: the copyist's mistakes can he corrected with ease. It is from a text such as this that the student of Syriac writings gains some idea of the literary and rheto-

1) *Julianos der Abtruennige, Syrische Erzaehlungen*, Leiden, 1880.

2) *Ueber den Syrischen Roman von Kaiser Julian* in *Z.D.M.G.* XXVIII pp. 263 et seq

3) Brit. Mus Add. 14641; see Wright, *Catalogue of the Syriac Manuscripts in the British Museum* p. 1042.

rical possibilities of the language — a consideration that is usually overlooked. The author writes with much warmth; and, saving a certain prolixity and verbosity, sustains the interest of the reader to the end.

Modern scholars are more apt to do justice to the Emperor Julian (331—363) than their predecessors have been. His attempt to restore Hellenism in some neo-Platonic form was bound to bring him into conflict with the Christian Church. Yet, it was part of this attempt to re-establish the principles of religious tolerance. His saying to the Christians "ut discordiis consopitis, quique, nullo vetante, religioni suae serviret intrepidus" is worthy of record; and throughout his short career he did not prove unfaithful to this principle. At a very early time, however, legends concerning Julian's cruelties to Christians grew up around his person and his acts — the product of the antagonism that he had aroused in the opposing camp. No record of such accusations is to be found either in Libanius or in Ammianus Marcellianus, his contemporaries, or in the writings of Julian himself. They make their appearance about one hundred years after the events took place with which they are supposed to deal. In course of time these accusations developed with the increase of the craving for the history of martyrs and saints. The student may consult Rendall, *The Emperor Julian,* London, 1879; C. J. NEUMAN's Edition of the Works of Julian translated into GERMAN, Leipzig, 1880; and especially Gaetano Negri, *Julian the Apostate,* translated by Duchess Litta-Visconti-Arese, London, 1905. A full bibliography is given in the article on Julian by K. BÖHMER in the *Real Encyclopädie für Protestantische Theologie,* Vol. IX, 609.

The following text contains the apocryphal history of the trials of a certain Eusebius, Bishop of Rome, which has been included in the original story as a specimen of the persecutions which the Christians had to suffer under the rule of the Emperor Julian called the Apostate. It has been pointed out that the whole Romance (aptly so called) was purported to do service in the conversion of the heathens to Christianity. Its historical value is therefore *nil*: as can best be seen from the facts that the EUSEBIUS mentioned as Bishop of Rome lived at the beginning of the fourth century, and that the Emperor JULIAN was never in Rome. The whole Romance originally contained: the history of Constantine and of his sons; the account of EUSEBIUS, Bishop of Rome, and his trials; and the history of Jovian during the reign of Julian. It seems curious that the text has survived in one manuscript only: it must have had more than ordinary vogue [1]). It may even be conjectured that a translation was

1) Another Julian Romance exists in the Syriac Ms. of the British Museum Rich 7192. According to NÖLDEKE it belongs to either the sixth or the seventh century. See *Z.D.M.G.* XXVIII, pp. 660—674.

made into Arabic; seeing that it evidently forms the basis for the legendary accounts of Julian in Muhammadan histories. This has been proven as regards al-Kalbī (died 819), al-Tabarī (born 838), *Ta'rīkh* I, p. 840; Ibn Wāḍiḥ al-Yaʿḳūbī (9th cent.) ed. Houtsma. I, p. 182; al-Masʿūdī (ca. 915) *Murūj al-Dhahab*. II, p. 323; Ḥamzah al-Iṣfahānī (ca. 961), *Annales* p. 74; Ibn al-Athīr (born 1160) *Kāmil*, I, p. 283; Abū al-Fidā (born 1273), *Hist. Anteislam.* ed. Fleischer, p. 84 — and, of course, the ubiquitous Bar Ebrāyā (born 1226), *Chronicon* ed. Bedjan p. 63 [1]).

In order to fit the selection into the space at the disposal of these handbooks, it has been necessary to shorten the text. I have done this by curtailing some of the longer speeches and letters and by omitting a large section near to the end: but in such a a manner as to preserve the continuity of the story. The passages selected are the following:

page	5	line	5 —	page	9	line	28
„	11	„	19 —	„	13	„	1
„	13	„	7 —	„	15	„	9
„	16	„	8 —	„	19	„	9
„	20	„	22 —	„	20	„	24
„	21	„	2 —	„	21	„	26
„	22	„	14 —	„	23	„	21

1) See Nöldeke *l. c.* p. 292; idem, *Geschichte der Perser*, p. 59; Wright, *A Short History of Syriac Literature*, p. 100.

page	23	line	28 —	page	24	line	17
„	24	„	26 —	„	27	„	9
„	31	„	8 —	„	31	„	16
„	32	„	9 —	„	32	„	18
„	33	„	13 —	„	33	„	19
„	36	„	24 —	„	37	„	14
„	38	„	2 —	„	39	„	2
„	56	„	28 —	„	59	„	4

The title I have taken from the subscription on p. 59, 6. A few necessary changes have been made in the text: nearly all upon the basis of the corrections proposed by Nöldeke and Hoffmann. The Romance has been reprinted from the same Ms. by Bedjan in his *Acta Martyrum et Sanctorum*, Vol. VI, pp. 218—297. I have compared his text with that given by Hoffmann for quite a number of pages: and the latter inspires me with much more confidence than does the former. Bedjan has evidently tried to bring up the old spelling to the modern Nestorian norm.

In place of a series of notes, I have determined upon a complete glossary of the words used. Extensive notes are apt to lighten the students work in translating. If he is compelled to look up the roots of the words he does not know, he prepares himself for his future use of Brockelmann's and Payne-Smith's dictionaries. Some peculiar expressions will be found translated under their chief catch-word. I have not added any vowels in the text, even where a difficulty or a real doubt exists. The chief words and forms will be found transliterated in the glossary. An occassional reference has been made to the second edition of Nöldeke's *Syrische Grammatik* in order to aid the student in his understanding of a passage. The Glossary has, of course, been kept within the closest possible bounds: and the temptation to go afield studiously repressed. Only such meanings as actually occur in the text have been noted. The development of these meanings from the root idea, as well as all questions of comparitive linguistics, have been left to the care of the teacher.

One of my students, Mr. Nicholas A. König, has kindly given me assistance in working out the glossary.

Richard J. H. Gottheil.

Columbia University, New York

February 1st 1906.

781097

ܬܫܥܝܬܐ ܕܕ̈ܝܢܘܗܝ ܕܐܘܣܒܝܘܣ ܦܦܐ ܐܦܝܣܩܘܦܐ
ܕܡܕܝܢܬܐ ܕܪܘܡܐ: ܒܝܘܡܝ ܝܘܠܝܢܘܣ ܛܪܘܢܐ
ܘܟܦܘܪܐ:

ܘܡܢ ܒܬܪ ܕܫܠܡ ܚܝܐ ܕܩܘܣܛܢܛܝܢܘܣ ܡܠܟܐ ܡܗܝܡܢܐ ܘܪܚܡ ܠܡܫܝܚܐ: ܘܐܬܬܢܝܚ ܠܘܬ ܡܪܗ ܕܡܠܟܐ. ܘܐܬܬܘܣܦ ܥܠ ܐܒ̈ܗܘܗܝ; ܘܫܒܩ ܠܗ ܫܡܐ ܛܒܐ ܘܕܘܟܪܢܐ ܕܠܥܠܡ. ܒܬܪܗ ܒܟܠܗܘܢ ܕܐܬܝܗܒ ܫܘܒܚܐ. ܘܩܡ ܒܬܪܗ ܒܡܠܟܘܬܐ ܝܘܠܝܢܘܣ ܪܫܝܥܐ ܘܒܝܫܐ ܗܘ ܐܢܫܐ ܕܒܝܫܘܬܗ ܘܡܟܫܦܢܘܬܐ ܕܫܐ̈ܕܐ. ܫܪܝ ܒܐܠܗܐ ܡܒܥܕܘ. ܘܗܦܟ ܡܢ ܡܫܝܚܝܘܬܐ ܫܪܝܪܬܐ ܕܠܗ ܐܚܝܕ ܗܘܐ ܡܢ ܛܠܝܘܬܗ ܘܕܓܠ ܒܡܫܝܚܗ ܘܗܦܟ ܡܢ ܫܪܪܗ. ܘܐܙܠ ܒܬܪ ܦܬܟܪܘܬܐ ܕܫܐ̈ܕܐ: ܘܐܬܛܦܝܣ ܠܡܫ̈ܡܫܢܘܗܝ ܘܐܬܕܒܪ ܠܡܨܒܝܢܘܗܝ ܘܩܪܒ ܘܐܬܬܟܠ ܒܚܝܠܗ ܕܫܐ̈ܕܐ ܘܡܫܬܡܥ ܗܘܐ ܠܦܬܟܪ̈ܐ: ܫܪܝ ܡܢ ܡ̈ܠܟܐ ܚܢܦܐ ܕܗܘܘ ܩܕܡܘܗܝ. ܘܫܪܝ ܕܒܚܐ ܠܦܬܟܪ̈ܐ. ܘܦܩܕ ܕܢܬܦܬܚܘܢ ܒܝܬ ܦܬܟܪ̈ܐ ܘܢܬܒܢܘܢ ܚܠܝܬܗܘܢ:

1

2

ܘܬܬܒܥܘܢ ܦܬܓܡܐ ܘܫܬܟܚܘܢ ܒ̈ܠܫܢܐ. ܘܬܬܝܩܪܘܢ
ܒܝܬ ܒܢܝ̈ܢܫܬܐ ܕܡ̈ܠܟܘܬܐ ܬܒ̈ܝܠ ܕܒܝܕܝ̈ܟܘܢ ܗ̈ܘܘ،
ܘܦܫܩ ܒܝܘ̈ܡܝ ܡ̈ܠܟܐ ܕܪ̈ܗܘܡܝܐ ܕܡܢ ܩܕܡܝܗܘܢ.
ܘܐܬܦܪܣ ܘܐܫܬܘܠܛ ܥܠ ܥܕ̈ܬܗ ܕܡܫܝܚܐ. ܘܢܦܩ
ܠܒܢ̈ܝܗܘܢ ܘܗܘܐ ܬܫܡܫܬܗܘܢ ܘܐܫܪ ܘܓܒܐ ܐܢܝ.
ܘܫܕܐ ܠܐܦܝܣܩܘܦ̈ܐ ܠܐܟܣܘܪܝܐ ܡܢ ܟܘܪ̈ܣܝܬܗܘܢ:
ܘܐܟܠ ܒܡܫܟܢܐ ܡܫܝܚܐ ܕܐܠܗܐ. ܘܐܪܕܦܗ ܒܟܠ
ܒܪ ܕܝܢܐ ܕܟܐܢܘܬܐ. ܘܠܐ ܝܗܒ ܠܗ ܐܠܗܐ
ܕܢܫܠܛ ܘܢܥܒܕ ܒܡܠܟܘܬܗ. ܡܛܠ ܒܪ ܐܪܕܘܗ ܡܢ
ܫܢܝܐ. ܘܒܬܪ ܡܫܝܚܘܬܐ ܕܩܕܡܘܗܝ. ܕܗܢ ܬܐܪܝܟ
ܠܗ ܓܒ ܘܬܒܥ ܡܫܝܚܘܬܐ ܕܢܦܫܗܘܢ: ܒܢ̈ܫܬܐ
ܒܪ ܦܘܠܘܣ̈ܬܐ ܐܦܠ ܠܬܒܥܘܢ ܕܐܠܗܐ ܗܘ
ܡܢܐ ܫܢܝܐ. ܘܦܪܥ ܐܠܗܐ ܒܒܥܘܗܝ ܒܢ̈ܫܐ
ܒܟܐܢܘܬܐ. ܘܗܘܐ ܐܟܙܢܐ ܒܐܪܥܐ ܕܟܠܒܝܐ.
ܐܝܟ ܕܗܘ ܗܘܐ ܐܬܝܗܒ ܠܒܢܘܗܝ ܟܘܫܪܐ ܕܐܠܗܐ
ܐܘܣܒܝܣ ܐܦܣܩܘܦܐ ܦܠܣܛܝܢܐ ܕܩܣܪܝܐ ܕܪܗܘܡܝܐ.
ܟܕ ܡܐܟ ܗܘܐ ܘܡܬܟܪܝܢ ܡܕܒܪܗܘܢ: ܬ̈ܫܥܐ ܒܢܝ
ܠܐ ܕܒܘ̈ܢܝ. ܘܫܪܪܐ ܘܐܘܠܨܢܐ ܕܡܫܠܡܢܐ ܕܟܠ
ܐܦ̈ܣܩܘܦܝ. ܐܫܬܟܚ ܠܗ ܠܗܢܐ ܗܟܢܐ ܬܚܝܬܗ
ܢܟܝ̈ܢܐ. ܘܠܐ ܐܬܬܣܝܡ ܐܘ ܐܬܒܣܪ ܡܢ ܡܫܝܪܘܬܐ
ܕܫ̈ܢܝܗܘܢ. ܘܗܘܒܐ ܒܪ ܕܒܪ ܬܫܥܝܢ ܘܫܒܥ ܫ̈ܢܝܢ

ܐܝܬܘܗܝ܇ ܗܘܐ ܗܢܐ ܩܕܡܝ̇. ܒܪ ܡܐܡܪ ܒܐܠܗܘܬܐ ܕܡܕܒܪܢܘܬܐ. ܘܟܗܢܐ ܕܠܗ ܝܘܩܪܐ ܕܡܫܝܚܘܬܐ. ܠܐ ܐܬܛܪܦ܇ ܡܢ ܝܩܪ̈ܗ. ܐܦ ܠܐ ܐܫܬܐܠ ܡܢ ܡܕܒܪܢܘܬܐ ܐܠܐ ܐܝܟ ܕܠܡܠܟܐ ܫܠܝܛܐ: ܡܟܐ ܕܡܐܡܪ ܥܠ ܬܘܩܦܐ ܕܢ̈ܝܫܘܗܝ. ܗܟܢܐ ܢܦܩ ܒܗ ܒܐܠܗܘܬܗ ܫܠܝܛܐܝܬ ܘܫܠܝܛܐܝܬ ܘܢܦܠ ܫܡܝܐ ܠܒܢܝܐ ܘܢܚܫܐ. ܘܡܢܐ܇ ܠܟܠܠܐ ܕܡܕܒܪܢܘܬܗ. ∴ ܗܘ ܡܘ̇ܕܝܐ ܘܡܕܡܐ ܕܐܫܟܚ ܒܦܘܪܩܢܗ ܕܐܕܡ. ܐܝܟ ܐܠܗܘܬܐ ܫܠܝܛܐ. ܗܘ ܫܪܝܐ ܦܬܚ ܐܡܨܥܝܢܐ ܕܐܬܠܛܦܘܬܐ. ܐܝܟ ܕܠܒܫܐ ܗܘ̣ܐ ܕܡܬܚܬܐ ܘܬܫܘܫܬܐ ܠܒܬܐ ܠܐܝܠܝܢ ܕܐܬܝܢ ܒܬܪܗ. ܕܢܪܘܢ ܒܚܘ̈ܒܘܗܝ ܘܢܡܪܘܢ ܒܐܬܠܛܦܘܬܗ. ܚܢܢ ܗܘ̣ܐ ܠܢ ܒܪܚܡܘܗܝ ܘܡܠܝܦ ܒܡܠܘܗܝ. ܘܫܠܛ ܒܡܠܬܗ. ܘܗܕܪ ܒܢܝܚܘܬܗ. ܘܐܢܗܪ ܒܝܘ̈ܠܦܢܘܗܝ܇ ܘܬܪܥܗ ܒܢ̈ܝܫܘܗܝ܇ ܒܡܫܪܪܘܬܐ ܕܠܢܝ ܕܡܫܡܠܝܬܐ ܕܠܒܡܐ. ܦܠܚ ܪܕܐ ܗܘ̣ܐ. ܘܒܡܦܩܬܐ ܕܡܫܡܠܝܬܐ ܠܢܝ ܕܦܘܠܘܦܬܐ ܘܡܫܘܫܪܘܬܐ ܘܡܫܪܪܘܬܐ ܡܠܝܐܝܬ ܡܕܪܫ ܗܘ̣ܐ. ܘܒܡܫܡܠܝܬܐ ܒܐܝܬܐ ܕܒܪܝܬܐ ܠܐܢܫܘ̈ܬܐ ܡܬܗܪ ܗܘ̣ܐ. ܕܡܬܥܪܐ ܕܝܢ ܘܫܡܝܢܐ ܡܢ ܟܠܗܝܢ. ܐܦ ܒܡܫܡܠܝܘܬܐ ܐܠܗܝܬܐ ܕܠܐ ܗܟܐ ܡܫܡܠ ܗܘ̣ܐ. ܘܟܠܗ ܒܟܠܗ ܡܬܪܥܐ.

ܗܘܐ ܠܘܝܘܡܗ ܐܦ ܠܝܪ̈ܘܬܗ̇. ܠܡܬܗܪ ܕܝܢ ܘܠܡܬܕܡܪܘ. ܕܟܕ ܒܠܒܗܘܢ ܠܓܡܪ ܗ̇ܘܐ ܘܡܣܬܟܠ: ܗ̇ܘ ܗܢܐ ܣܒܐ ܡܒܪܟܐ. ܘܡܕܡ ܠܐ ܚܣܪ ܗ̇ܘܐ ܡܢ ܡܠܝܘܬܗ̇. ܕܒܟܠ ܡܬܝܢ ܗܘܐ ܘܡܬܕܒܪ ܕܢܒܥܐ ܢܦܩ ܠܗ ܡܘܬܪ̈ܢܐ ܐܠܗ̈ܝܐ. ܕܠܐ ܡܣܬܝܟܝܢ. ܟܕ ܐܦ ܠܐ ܠܓܡܪ ܫܒܩܬ ܢܦܫܗ ܡܢ ܦܘܠܚܢܐ ܕܙܕܝܩܘܬܐ. ܕܒܡܟܐ ܠܢܫܡܬܐ ܐܚܪܬܐ. ܘܟܕ ܡܢ ܟܕܘ ܣܒܐ ܡܪܝܒ. ܗܘܐ ܓܝܪ ܥܘܠܡܢܐ ܕܝܪ̈ܘܬܗ: ܘܟܠ ܪܫ ܐܘܪܚܐ ܕܡܐܠܬܗ ܡܐܟ ܗ̇ܘܐ. ܗ̇ܘ ܠܓܡܪ ܠܐ ܫܠܐ ܗ̇ܘܐ ܡܢ ܕܢܪܕܐ ܒܫܡܗ ܡܢ ܡܘܬܪ̈ܢܐ ܕܕܒܪ̈ܘܗܝ: ܗܕܐ ܓܝܪ ܡܨܥܝܘܬܐ ܗܘܬ ܠܗ ܒܝܢ ܣܒܘܬܗ. ܕܙܘ̈ܕܐ ܟܠ ܙܘ̈ܕܐ ܢܦܘܩ ܠܗ ܠܐܘܪܚܐ ܢܓܝܪܬܐ ܕܡܐܠܬܗ. ܘܟܕ ܫܒܩܬ ܒܗ ܬܓܘܪܬܐ ܪܘܚܢܝܬܐ. ܒܕܡܘܬ ܟܦܢܐ ܘܨܗܝܐ ܒܫܕܘܬܗ ܗܘ ܒܠܒܗ̇. ܘܗܕ ܒܣܒܝܒܘܬܗ ܡܒܝܢܬܐ ܠܒܬܐ ܕܡܕܒܪܢܘܬܐ. ܕܠܗ̇ ܡܬܝܐܒ ܗܘܐ ܡܢ ܠܠܘܬܗ. ܘܪܘܡ ܓܝܪ ܡܪܝܗ ܒܝܒܘܬܐ. ܟܕ ܠܒܝܢ ܟܠ ܒܬܦܗ ܡܠܐܐ ܕܬܐܓܘܪܬܗ. ܘܒܫܪܪܐ ܗܘܢ ܬܓܪܐ ܚܕܝܡܐ ܕܠܘܫܬܝܢ. ܕܣܦܩ ܒܝܕܒܬܗ ܕܝܬܬܓܪ ܬܢܢܐ ܠܘܝܡܗ. ܒܓܕܐ ܠܓܒܐ ܘܒܫܪܪܐ. ܕܟܦ̈ܐܐ ܟܠܝܬܐ ܐܝܬ ܠܗ ܕܢܟܒ ܠܡܪܗ ܚܘܫܒܢ

ܟܪܝܐ ܕܐܓܚܟ ܠܗ. ܘܡܠܐ ܠܚܕܘܬܐ ܘܫܒܪܐ. ܕܡܢ ܛܦܪܐ ܫܪܝ، ܒܦܘܠܚܢܐ ܕܡܪܗ. ܘܒܚܝܠ ܚܘܒܐ ܕܬܠܡܝܕܘܬܗ ܣܒܠ ܢܝܪܐ ܕܢܡܘܣܗ ܕܡܫܝܚܐ ܘܠܐ ܐܬܒܛܠ ܡܢ ܦܘܠܚܢܐ ܕܡܪܗ: ܘܟܕ ܬܘܒ ܪܒܐ ܬܠܡܝܕܘܗܝ ܕܬܠܡܝܕܘܬܐ. ܘܫܡܥܢ ܒܠܗܘܢ، ܦܫܝܛ ܕܫܒܚܘܬܐ. ܠܐ ܐܬܟܢܝ ܒܡܠܐ ܕܦܘܠܚܢܗ: ܕܐܝܬܝ ܡܢ ܕܒܬܠܡܝܕܘܬܗ ܐܬܝܪ ܦܘܠܚܢܐ ܕܒܐܝܕܘܬܗ ܒܝܢ ܫܒܝܬܗ. ܘܟܕ ܪܡ ܠܗ ܘܓܠܐ ܐܦ̈ܝܗܝ. ܡܫܚܠ ܡܢ ܡܪܗ ܐܓܪܐ ܕܦܘܠܚܢܗ. ܘܡܒܣܐ ܐܝܬ ܠܗ ܕܢܠܒ. ܠܡܢ ܕܠܐ ܚܣܡ ܥܠ ܡܘܠܟܢܗ ܕܡܠܟܐ̈ ܕܡܒܪ̈ܘܗܝ، ܠܟܢ̈ܪܐ ܘܫܡܪ̈ܬܘܗܝ، ܒܣ̈ܢܝܐ ܘܪ̈ܓܝܫܘܗܝ، ܬܫ̈ܡܫܬܐ ܘܡܗܝܢ ܡܟܪܝܢ ܥܠܝܗ ܡ̈ܠܟܘܗܝ: ܕܠܐ ܗܝܠ ܢܦܘܫ ܠܝ ܡܢ ܬܫܡܫܬܐ ܕܡܫܡܫܘܬܗ ܠܒܬܐ. ܕܗܘܐ ܒܪܢܫܐ ܪܘܚܢܐ. ܘܗܘܐ ܗܝܟܠܐ ܠܡܠܟܐ ܐܠܗܝܐ ܕܕܘܒܪ̈ܘܗܝ: ܘܠܚ̈ܫܐ ܘܠܥ̈ܢܕܐ ܕܡܕܒ̈ܪܢܘܗܝ: ܘܠܒܢ̈ܝܬܐ ܟܠܐ ܐܠܗ̈ܝܬܐ ܕܡܪܝܢ ܐܬܡܠܠ. ܢܐܬܐ ܡܚܝܠ ܚܝܢ ܫܘܪܝܗ ܕܬܫܒܚܬܗ. ܕܒܦܘܪܣܬܐ ܢܫܡܥ ܐܠܗܝܐ ܕܡܕܒܪܢܘܬܗ ⁘

ܘܗܫܐ ܡܢ ܒܬܪ ܕܡܢܬ ܡܘܦܠܝܣ ܐܝܟ ܕܐܬܚܙܝ ܡܢ ܠܚܠ. ܐܬܚܫܒ ܢܠܘܢܘܣ ܠܦܪܘܣܐ ܒܚܝܠܐ ܡܠܟܐܝܐ ܠܡܚܘܬ ܠܬܪܘܕܐ. ܡܢ ܐܬܪܘܬܐ ܚܠܝܐ

6

ܕܓܠܝܘܣ ܕܒܗܘܢ ܡܨܠܝܢ ܗܘܘ. ܐܝܟ ܕܢܚܕܬ ܡܠܟܘܬܐ ܥܠ ܟܘܪܣܝܐ ܕܪ̈ܗܘܡܝܐ. ܘܢܗܘܐ ܐܘܛܩܪܛܘܪ ܥܠ ܟܠܗ ܐܘܚܕܢܐ ܕܪ̈ܗܘܡܝܐ. ܘܟܕ ܐܝܟ ܛܘܒܢܐ ܐܘܣܒܝܘܣ ܒܗܠܝܢ: ܘܐܒܠܐ. ܘܐܝܬܪ̈ ܡܢ ܩ̈ܣܛܢܐ ܥܠ ܛܪܘܢܐ ܕܗܘ ܡܓܠܝܢ. ܘܫ ܒܥܕܢܗ ܘܡܠܝܐܝܬ ܐܬܬܢܚ ܒܠܒܗ. ܘܐܬܬܢܚ ܘܐܡܪ. ܘܝ ܠܝ ܕܓܒܪ ܐܚܘܪܐ ܡܢ ܚܪ̈ܬܐ ܘܡܬܬܚܡܒ ܡܘܕܝܢ ܠܡܠܟܐ. ܘܡܢܟܢ ܠܒܢܝܐ ܘܒܢܝܢ ܠܛܪܘܦܝܐ. ܐܬܬܟܝܡ ܗܘܐ ܠܗ ܟܝܪ ܛܒܥܐ ܕܢܦܩܘܬܗ ܕܗܢܐ ܫܢܝܐ. ܘܐܡܠܟܬ ܗܘܬ ܠܗ ܒܠܒܗ، ܛܒ ܒܪܘܢܬܐ ܥܠ ܢܦܫܐ ܕܐܠܗܐ ܘܢܫܢܐܝܬ ܒܕܡܘܬ ܐܪܡܝܐ ܡܟܒܟܐ ܗܘܐ ܠܗܘܢ ܠܬܠܡܝܕܐ ܕܪ̈ܘܦܝܢܐ ܕܒܢܝܢ. ܘܡܬܬܚܝܢ ܗܘܐ ܠܗܘܢ ܒܪ ܐܢܫ. ܫܠܝܚ ܠܗ ܠܡܠܟܘܬܗ ܕܐܬܓܠܝܬ ܡܢ ܡܕܒܪܢܘܬܗܘܢ ܡܡܪ̈ܚܢܐ ܕܗܝܡܢܘܬܗܘܢ ܘܡ̈ܫܝܚܝܗ ܕܒܕܬܐ. ܐܚܪܢܐ ܒܫܢܝܐ ܕܒܠܝܬܗܘܢ ܒܐܫܕܪܐ ܡܠܝܬ ܒܩ̈ܒܠܐ. ܘܒܩܪܬܗܘܢ ܡܢܝܢ ܡܚܪܗ ܕܢܦܠܝܬܐ ܘܫ̈ܢܝܢܗ ܕܢܩܘܫܬܐ: ܘܦܠܝܓܘܬܗ ܒܗܘܢܐ ܕܡܬܡܢܝܘܬܗܘܢ܆ ܘܫܕܝܬܗܘܢ ܒܗ ܕܪ̈ܒܐ ܛܒܥܐ ܕܡܫܦܪܢܘܬܗܘܢ: ܘܡܢܗ ܬܒܗ ܦܐܪܐ ܒܬܠܬܝܢ ܘܒܫܬܝܢ ܘܒܡܐܐ. ܘܗܘܐ ܐܝܟ ܗܢܐ ܕܦܠܚܝܢ ܘܡܫܝܢ ܘܡܒܪܝܢ܆ ܛܒܥܐ ܒܬܒܠ.

ܒܐܝܢ ܗܠܝܢ ܒ̈ܢܬ ܩ̈ܠܐ ܚܫ̈ܝܫܬܐ ܦܠܓ̈ܝܐܬܐ ܘܕܕܡܝܢ ܠܗܝܢ. ܡܬܬܒܪ ܗ̤ܘܐ ܠܗܘܢ ܦܘܣܒܐ ܐܘܣܒܣ ܠܛܝܛܘܣ ܘܕܘܡܛܝܢܘܣ ܡ̈ܠܟܐ ܕܪ̈ܗܘܡܝܐ. ܡܢ ܬܘܪܘܬܐ ܕܠܟܘܢ ܘܡܫܐ ܕܪܒܢܘܗ̇. ܘܒܪ ܐܦܣܝ̈ܢ ܡܠܠ ܪ̈ܒܢܘܗ ܒܝܕ ܕܗ̈ܕܐ ܕܒ̈ܢܘܗܝ. ܒܕܡܘܬ ܪ̈ܒܢܐ ܕܐܝܠܐ ܕܒܐܝܟ ܠܗ ܟܠ ܡܕܪܒܝܬܗ: ܐܡܬܝ ܕܡܬܬܣܝܡ ܕܐܝܟܐ ܕܝܫܘܥ ܦܓܪܗ. ܘܫܪܐ ܐܠܐ ܒܗ̇ ܒܒܠܐ ܘܒܢܝܢܗ̇ ܠܗܬܦ. ܗܒܢܐ ܒܗܪܐ ܕܡܘܬܐ ܐܦ ܫܒܠܐ ܡܕܒܪܢܐ. ܒܕ ܫܡܒ ܟܠ ܡܐܬܝܬܗ ܕܗܢܐ ܡܣܝܒܐ. ܒܒܠܠܘܬܐ ܦܠܓܐܬܐ ܫܕܪ ܒܢܫܗ ܠܗܬܗ ܠܟܠܗ ܡܢܡܐ ܕܒܕܬܐ. ܡܢ ܪܒܐ ܘܒܕܡܐ ܠܒܘܪܐ. ܘܐܝܟ ܕܠܩ̈ܢܝܐ ܚܒ̈ܝܒܐ ܡܪܬܐ ܗܘܐ ܠܗܘܢ ܒܕ ܐܡ̈ܪ. ܚܘ ܩ̈ܛܝܢ ܐܘܕܗܘ ܒܦܣܩܘܢ ܘܐܫܬܪܘ ܒܗ̇ܝܡܢܘܬܟܘܢ ܘܫܡܫܘܢ ܒܫܪܪܘܢ ܘܗܘܘ ܠܒ̈ܢܝܐ ܘܚܠܝܬܐ. ܕܐܝܟܐ ܓܒܪ ܕܝܬܒ ܕܢܫܬܠܠ ܟܠܗ. ܘܫܘܝܐ ܐܝܬ ܠܗ ܕܢܦܘܩ ܟܠ ܟܕܬܐ. ܚܝܘ ܕܠܡܐ ܬܬܪܦܘܢ ܡܢ ܫܪܪܘܢ ܘܬܬܦܠܓ ܠܟܘܢ ܒܢܘܫܘܢ. ܡܠܠ ܗܘ ܓܒܪ ܕܒܝܐ ܘܦܠܓ ܕܒܪ. ܘܫܒܠ ܠܗ ܫܘܠܡܐ ܢܘܫܘܢ ܠܐ ܓܒܪ ܡܪܦܐ ܐܠܗܐ ܐܝܕܐ ܒܡܕܒܪܢܘܬܗ. ܕܒܕܡܗ ܡܢܪܐ ܕܒܝܐ ܠܗ. ܘܠܐ ܫܟܡ ܠܗ̇ ܠܓܒܪ

8

ܒܐܝܕܝ̈ ܕܐܒܐ. ܐܦ ܓܝܪ ܢܗܘܐ ܕܡܠܐ ܘܒܢܝܐ ܢܬܛܠܠ ܦܪܘܩܐ ܠܢܦܫܐ ܟܠ ܡܠܟܘܬܗ̈ ܠܡܪܕܘܬܗ̈ ܟܠ ܕܢܦܩܝܢ. ܐܠܐ ܬܗܘܐ ܒ̈ܢܝ ܡܗܝܡܢܐ ܘܫܪ̈ܪܐ ܠܝ. ܕܟܡܘܟܐ ܕܫܘܪܝܗ ܒܟܠ ܫܘܠܡܗ. ܠܐ ܓܝܪ ܡܫܬܘܕܐ ܐܢܐ ܐܠܗܐ ܚܪܢܐ ܡܢ ܒܪܝܬܗ. ܐܠܐ ܒܠܒܝܢ ܒ̈ܢܘܗܝ ܚܠܝܦ ܠܦܠܚܘܬܐ. ܐܦ ܒܢܝܢ ܡܪܕܘܬܗ. ܐܡܬܝ ܓܝܪ ܠܐ ܦܪܘܩܝ ܒܢܝܢ ܢܦܫܢ. ܠܐ ܗܘܝܠ ܬܬܠܒܫܘܢ ܐܘ ܬܬܪܗܒܘܢ ܡܢ ܦܠܚܐ ܕܢܦܩܬܗ ܕܗܘܝܐ ܦܪܘܩܢܝ. ܕܗܘܝܢ ܡܬܬܪܝܡ ܘܡܫܬܠܡ: ܘܡܢܝܪ ܟܠܠ ܘܠܝܬܘܗܝ. ܘܐܒܝ ܘܐܬܒܠܦ ܕܒܪܝܗ. ܘܕܒܪܝܐ ܕܒܝܢ ܒܗ ܫܪܪܐ ܒܡܕܝܢܘܬܗ̈. ܠܒܠܡ ܠܐ ܡܬܡܠܠ ܒܒܪܝܬܐ. ܠܡܫܝܚܐ ܗܘܝܠ ܘܠܡܪܢ. ܐܝܟ ܐܢܫܐ ܓܡܝܪܐ ܘܫܪ̈ܪܐ. ܐܡܬܝ ܕܢܩ̈ܘܒܐ ܒܕܝܢ ܒܠܝܒܘ ܒܪܝܐܝܬ. ܕܒܕܡܘܬ ܕܗܘܐ ܠܒܐ ܕܒܒܘܪܐ ܡܢܗܘܐ ܫܘܦܪܐ ܕܦܐܝܘܬܗ: ܘܬܗܪ̈ܝܢ ܒܗ ܚܝ̈ܘܗܝ. ܗܒܢܐ ܒܒܘܪܐ ܕܢܩ̈ܘܒܐ ܡܬܒܚ̈ܝܢ ܠܓܢ̈ܝܐ. ܘܒܢ ܒܘܟܐ ܕܡܫܝܒܪܘܬܗܘܢ ܡܬܝܒܝܢ ܫܪ̈ܝܪܐ. ܕܠܐ ܓܝܪ ܐܓܘܢܐ ܘܠܐ ܢܨܚܢܐ ܘܠܐ ܕܒܘܩܐ. ܐܦܠܐ ܠܠܒܐ ܘܠܒܘܬܐ ܒܒܘܣܝܗ ܕܡܫܒܪܢܘܬܗܘܢ ܡܬܘܠܦܝܢ ܠܓܢ̈ܝܐ. ܘܫܘܠܡܐ ܕܪܗܛܗܘܢ. ܡܢܐ ܕܐܡܪ ܫܘܠܡ ܢܨܚܢܐ.

ܠܐ ܢܦܠܘܢ ܠܗ ܠܐܬܠܝܦܬܐ ܕܫܡܝܐ ܕܐܬܠܝܦܘܬܗ: ܐܝܟ ܒܡܘܬܗ ܕܫܠܝܘܬܗ ܒܐܓܘܢܐ ܠܐ ܢܣܒܘܢ. ܐܦܠܐ ܠܬܪܘܡܝܢܐ ܕܫܡܝܐ ܕܬܪܘܡܝܢܘܬܗ. ܐܝܟ ܒܡܘܬܗ ܕܡܫܒܪܢܘܬܗ ܒܐܘܠܨܢܘܗܝ ܠܐ ܢܣܒܘܢ. ܘܫܡܥܒ ܠܫܠܝܚܐ ܕܐܡܪ ܦܘܠܘܣ)[1]. ܕܐܘܠܨܢܐ ܡܫܒܪܢܘܬܐ ܠܗ ܡܥܒܕܐ ܗܘ. ܘܡܫܒܪܢܘܬܐ ܒܘܚܢܐ. ܘܒܘܚܢܐ ܣܒܪܐ. ܣܒܪܐ ܕܝܢ ܠܐ ܡܒܗܬ. ܐܝܟ ܐܢܫܐ ܗܢܐ ܕܫܪܝܪܐ ܠܗܘܢ: ܘܬܒܠܝܢ ܕܐܝܬ ܠܗܘܢ ܣܒܪܐ ܕܠܐ ܡܒܗܬ. ܫܪܘ ܡܛܠܗܘܢ ܡܐܢܝܘܬܐ ܘܪܦܝܘܬܐ ܘܡܘܬܒ ܪܚܡܢܐ. ܘܐܚܝܕܘ ܕܪܐ ܒܗ ܚܦܝܛܘܬܐ ܘܬܒܪܘ ܟ̈ܘܒܫܘܗܝ ܘܒܝܢܝܐ ܪܘܚܢܐ ܕܩܢܝܢ ܐܢܘܢ. ܐܬܬܒܥܘ ܒܗ ܦܘܠܚܢ ܘܫܡܘ ܢܐܦܘܗܝ: ܠܗܘܢ ܠܒܪ ܐܝܟ ܒܐܫܐ. ܘܠܒܘܢ ܦܐܝܐ ܠܓܒܪܘܬܐ. ܕܗܝ ܗܘ ܫܘܐܬܗ ܕܒܪܬܐ ܪܫ ܬܠܡ̈ܝܕܐ ܠܬܠܘܢ ܠܦܩܣܐ ܕܐܬܠܝܦܘܬܐ. ܘܕܪܫܘܢ ܠܦ̈ܩܬܗ ܕܐܓܘܢܝܣܛܘܬܐ. ܘܠܝܬ ܠܗ ܠܫܝܐ ܠܓܒܪ ܕܢܣܒ ܡܢܗܘܢ ܕܒܘܬܐ. ܕܫܪܝܪܐ ܕܙܕܝܩܘܬܐ ܠܒܢܝܢ ܐܢܘܢ ܘܒܢܝܢܐ ܪܘܚܢܐ ܡܚܝܘ ܪܒܢܝܢܘܢ ܀

ܘܒܬܪ ܬܘܒ ܙܒܢܐ ܗܘܐ ܠܦܘܠܝܢܐ ܐܘܣܒܝܣ

1) Romans V, 4.

10

ܕܢܬܬܘܚ ܡܠܬܗ ܥܠ ܡܠܦܢܘܬܗ. ܐܦܝܣܩܘܦܘܣ ܡܫܡܫܢܐ ܠܗ ܦܩܕܗ ܘܐܡܪ ܠܗ. ܐܙܠ. ܗܒ ܠܗ̇ ܥܠܝܐ ܠܬܠܬܝܢ ܡܢ ܗܢܐ ܘܐܝܟ ܕܐܬܒܥܝ. ܐܬܬܥܝܪ ܡܢ ܫܢܬܐ ܘܣܪܗܒ ܐܙܠܘܢܐ. ܘܡܢ ܒܬܪ ܡܫܬܟܚܬܘܢ ܠܕܪܓܐ ܡܥܠܝܐ ܕܡܫܡܫܢܘܬܐ ܫܘܬ. ܦܘܩܕܢܗ ܕܝܢ ܕܐܠܗܐ. ܗܘ ܒܝܕܗ ܒܐܝܠܝܢ ܕܢܦܩ. ܘܚܪ ܒܗ ܒܫܡܫܐ ܗܘ ܚܒܝܒܐܝܬ. ܘܫܐܠܗ ܘܐܡܪ ܠܗ. ܡܢܘ ܒܪ، ܦܬܓܡܟ ܗܢܐ: ܦܢܝ ܠܗ ܕܝܢ ܦܬܓܡܐ ܐܦܝܣܩܘܦܘܣ ܡܫܡܫܢܗ ܒܕ ܐܡܪ. ܡܫܬܘܕܐ ܠܟ ܐܫܬܘܕܝܬ ܥܠ ܬܪܥܗ ܒܒܐ ܕܒܝܬܐ. ܡܛܠ ܦܘܠܚܢܐ ܕܡܫܡܫܢܘܬܟ. ܘܚܕ ܡܢ ܦܠܚܐ ܪ̈ܚܡܢܐ ܕܫܡܗ ܐܘܪܘܦܝܣ. ܡܫܐܠ ܗܘܐ ܡܛܠ ܡܠܐܟܝܢ ܘܫܐܠܐ. ܘܗܘ ܗܢܐ ܚܕ ܡܢ ܡܫ̈ܡܫܢܘܗܝ ܕܦܪܘܫܐ ܐܝܬܘܗܝ. ܐܝܟ ܕܝܠܦܬ ܡܢ ܐܝܠܝܢ ܕܚܙܘܗܝ. ܘܐܝܬ ܒܗܘܢ ܐܚܪܢܐ ܐܬܪ̈ܘܢܐ. ܘܦܘܪܣܐ ܡܢ ܒܡܬܪ̈ܗ ܕܢܦܫܬܐ. ܘܥܠ ܐܬܪ̈ܘܗܝ ܡܫ̈ܡܫܢܘܬܗ ܕܡܠܟܐ ܕܪ̈ܘܚܐ ܠܡܫܡܫܘܬܟ. ܘܥܠ ܐܝ̈ܕܘܗܝ، ܕܐܝܪܘܦܘܣ. ܚܪܒܗ ܕܦܘܪܣܐ ܒܕ ܫܡܥܦܠܐ. ܝܗ̄ܒ ܠܒܪ ܕܢܦܠ ܠܟܘ ܡܢ ܬܪܥܗ ܒܪܐ ܕܒܝܬܐ ܘܠܐ ܢܣܒܬ ܠܗ. ܒܢܦ̈ܪ، ܬܪܥܗ ܒܪ ܕܠܝܬܗ ܒܪ ܕܠܝܐ ܚܝܘܬܟ ܒܥܠܝܢ. ܬܫܪܬ

ܕܝܢ ܒܗܢܐ ܒܒܪܗ ܕܫܠܝܚܘܬܗ. ܕܐܝܟܢܐ ܣܓܠ ܒܦܣܩܗ. ܘܠܐ ܐܬܚܫܒܬ ܐܘ ܙܟܝ ܒܐܝܠܝܢ ܕܣܒܪܬ ܠܗ. ܐܦܠܐ ܐܬܚܝܪ، ܕܢܦܠ ܡܢ ܕܝܠܗ ܢܟܝܢ. ܘܗܘܐ ܚܐܪ ܒܕܒܝܠ ܠܦܘܪܢܝ. ܠܦܒܝܐ ܕܝܢ ܐܘܣܒܝܣ ܒܪ ܦܡܦܝܠܐ ܗܠܝܢ ܒܠܗܝܢ. ܠܐ ܐܬܪܗܒ. ܐܘ ܐܬܪܦܝ. ܡܣܘܟ ܗܘܐ ܓܝܪ ܘܣܘܐ. ܕܐܡܬܝ، ܢܬܦܬܚ ܠܗ ܬܪܥܐ ܕܡܫܝܚܝܘܬܐ. ܠܦܒܝܐ ܓܝܪ ܢܗܝܪ ܗܘܐ ܒܡܠܟܐ: ܠܐܝܠܝܢ ܕܨܒܘ ܠܡܗܪܐ ܒܗܝܡܢܘܬܐ. ܐܡܬܝ، ܕܢܦܪܐ ܗܘܐ ܒܣܘ̈ܪܕܘܬܗܘܢ ܘܡܬܗܪܝܢ ܒܢ̈ܝܫܝܫܘܗܝ. ܘܟܕ ܠܒ ܫܪܐ ܗܘܐ ܘܪܘܪ ܙܒܢܝܢ ܒܦܪܢܣܐ ܗܢܐ ܕܐܬܦܪܣ، ܠܗ ܣܓܝ ܗܘܐ ܚܫܐ ܥܠܝܠ ܒܪܒܝܗ. ܡܛܠ ܐܝܠܝܢ ܕܐܝܬ ܗܘܐ ܒܡܪܒܝܬܗ ܕܟܠܒܐ ܗܘܐ ܒܪܒܝܠ ܬܘܠܡܕܘܗܝ. ܒܕܠܐ ܡܦܣܐ ܗܘܐ. ܐܝܟܢܐ ܕܢܦܩܝܢ ܒܗ ܒܐܠܘܣܘܗܝ. ܘܟܕ ܚܙܐ ܠܡܪܒܝܬܗ. ܕܡܬܪܐ ܘܡܫܝܚܐ. ܐܝܟ ܐܝܕܗ ܘܫܬܡܗ ܠܟܠܗ ܡܝܬܐ ܕܪܒܘܬܐ. ܠܚܒܪܐ ܘܠܢ̈ܫܐ. ܘܡܠܐ ܠܒܠܗܘܢ. ܘܒܢܐ ܐܢܘܢ ܘܐܡܪ ܠܗܘܢ. ܐܬܠܒܒܘ ܒܢܝ ܘܠܐ ܬܕܚܠܘܢ ܘܐܬܕܟܪܘ ܕܐܝܠܝܢ ܡ̈ܠܐ ܡܠܠܬ ܠܟܘܢ. ܘܡܪܢ ܒܝ ܕܐܝܬ، ܗܟܢܐ ܒܪ ܬܫܒܚܝܢ ܓ̈ܒܝܢ ܘܬܘܪ ܡܢ ܕܡܬܪܚܩ ܐܢܫ ܠܟ̈ܠܗܐ ܡܪ̈ܕܐ ܡܢܐ ܕܗܘܐ. ܗܟܢܐ ܗܘܐ ܢܦܫ ܡܫܠܡܐ.

ܕܐܝܟܢܐ ܡܕܒܪܢܐ ܐܚܘܐ ܒܡܕܒܪܢܘܬܗ ܕܐܓܘܢܐ ܘܠܡܫܝܚܗ ܕܪܘܚܢܝ. ܘܢܦܩ ܒܗ ܫܘܪܝܐ ܘܫܘܠܡܐ ܕܪܘܚܢܝܐ ܕܒܪ̈ܘܦܛܝܢܐ. ܘܒܗ ܢܬܬܢܝܚ ܦܓܪܗ ܕܒܐܝܢܘܬܐ. ܘܬܪܒܝܐ ܐܠܗܐ ܠܒܢܝܗ. ܒܬܪ ܕܝܢ ܐܢܬܘܢ ܒܢ̈ܝ: ܫܘܘ ܝܚܝܕܝܐ ܦܓܥܐ ܝܗ̈ܒ ܐܠܗܝ̈. ܘܗܘܘ ܒܥܬܝܕ ܘܗܘܘ ܒܬܪܝܢ ܘܡܦܠܓܝܢ ܠܡܕܒܪܢܘܬܐ ܦܠܓܘܬܐ ܕܟܠ ܐܦ̈ܝ ܡܢܝܢܐ.

ܘܟܕ ܒܗܠܝܢ ܒܢ̈ܝܗ ܩ̈ܠܐ ܕܒܘܢܐ ܡܢܝܢ ܗܘܐ ܠܗ̇ ܠܡܪܒܝܢܘܬܗ. ܦܪܘܬܦܘܣ ܢܦ̈ܫ ܬܪܒܗ̇ ܕܒܕܝܬܐ ܒܠ ܒܠܗܝܗ ܘܐܡܪ ܠܗ. ܐܕܘܦܠܘܣ ܠܟ ܡܗܝܡܢܝܗ ܕܚܠܝܢܘܣ ܒܐܝ̈ܬܝ، ܒܒܕܝܟ ܥܠܝܟ ܠܫܒܝܚܘܬܟ. ܕܐܒܢ ܐܝܬ ܝܒܝܫܐ ܠܫܒܚܘܬܟ. ܕܒܝܫ ܘܠܟ ܐܫܬܡܥܟ ܐܝܠܝܢ ܕܐܫܬܠܝܛ ܕܐܡܪ ܠܟ. ܦܘܩܕ ܠܟ ܘܫܒܘܩ ܡܕܡܝܟ. ܘܐܢ ܬܘܒ ܐܝܬ ܠܟ ܝܒܝܫܐ ܕܡܕܡ ܒܫܐܐ ܗܢܐ ܕܒܝܫ ܐܦܠܘ ܠܗ̇ ܐܝܩܪܐ ܠܫܝܒܘܬܟ ܐܝܟ ܕܐܬܦܩܕܬ. ܐܦ ܗܕܐ ܠܟ ܬܘܒ ܕܠܟ ܗ̇ܝ. ܒܬܪ ܕܝܢ ܐܘܕܝܬ ܝܒܝܟ. ܐܘܫܦܝܫ ܕܝܢ ܦܘܠܘܣ ܐܡܪ̈ ܠܐܝܠܝܢ ܕܒܡܗ. ܕܠܐ ܒܢ̈ܝ ܢܒܠܘܢ ܦ̈ܠܓܘܬܐ. ܘܢܕܘܫܘܢ ܒܝܬܗ ܕܡܪܝܐ. ܢܬܠ ܢܦܫ ܕܝܠܝ ܢܦܘܩ ܠܬܘܡܗ. ܘܬܝܪܬܐܝܬ ܡܦܠܠ ܒܥ̈ܝܢܗ ܕܡܕܝܢܬܐ. ܘܢܐܠܦ ܡܢܘ ܝܒܝܫܗ ܕܡܫܒܚܐ. ܘܐܝܠܝܢ ܐܬܪ̈ܒܝ ܒܠ ܒܡܢ ܘܒܠ ܚ̈ܕܬ ܘܠܦܘܬ ܐܝܠܝܢ ܕܫܠܝܛ ܠܝ.

ܡܫܡܫܢܘܬܐ ܕܠܫܡܫܐ ܠܟܗܢܘܬܗ ܒܐܝ̈ܕܝ̣ ܫܠܝܚܘܗ̇ ܢܗܦܟ ܠܗ.

ܘܟܕ ܩܪܒ ܙ̇ܒܢܐ ܢܦܫܗ ܕܢܦܘܩ ܡܢ ܥܕܬܗ̇. ܐܚܕܬ ܚܡܟܡ̣ ܟܠܗ̇ ܡܪ̈ܟܒܝܬܗ. ܘܐܦ ܗ̣ܘܐ ܒܪܝ ܡܕܡܗ̇ ܕܥܕܬܐ. ܐܝܟ ܪ̇ܒ ܚܝܠܐ ܒܪ̈ܫܐ ܕܡܫܪ̈ܝܬܗ. ܗܘܝܢ ܗܘܘ ܕܝܢ ܐܝܠܝܢ ܕܐܬܠܘܘ ܠܗ ܘܢܦܩܘ ܥܡܗ ܡܢ ܥܕܬܐ: ܟܝܢܐ ܢܟܦܐ ܘܟܝܢܐ ܙ̇ܒܢܝܢ: ܒܢܫܐ ܕܡܠܟ̈ܐ ܘܕܫ̈ܢܐ: ܐܝܟ ܐܠܦ ܘܬܫܥܡܐܐ ܘܬܠܬܝܢ ܢܦܫܢ. ܘܗܕܐ ܗܘܬ ܘܪܒܘ ܪ̇ܒܝܢܗ̇ ܒܒܘܫܬܐ ܕܥܕܬܗ: ܘܬܪ̇ܐܝܬ ܥܠ ܪ̇ܒܢܐ ܫܠܝ̈ܚܐ ܕܩܕܡ ܗܘܘ. ܘܫܒ̇ܩ ܗܘܐ ܠܗܘܢ ܛܘܒܢܐ ܘܡܫܠܛ ܗܘܐ ܠܡܫܡܫܢܘܬܗܘܢ: ܘܟܕ ܗܠܝܢ ܪ̇ܒܢܐ ܟܪ̇ܝܐ ܗ̣ܘ ܘܡܕ̇ܒܪܢܘܬܗ ܠܛܘܒܢܐ ܟܪܝܐ ܕܥܕܬܐ. ܐܝܟ ܕܟܬܝܒ ܠܛܘܒܢܘܬܐ ܕܐܠܗܐ. ܘܗܘܐ ܦܐܝܐ ܐܬܢܨܚ ܥܠ ܦܪ̈ܨܘܦܗ ܕܐܘܣܒܝܣ ܛܘܒܢܐ. ܘܕܡ̈ܐ ܗܘܐ ܚܙܘܗ̣ ܠܚܝܘܐ ܕܡܠܐܟܐ. ܗܟܢܐ ܕܗܕܐ ܚܝܘܗܝ، ܐܕܘܡܝܛܐ. ܬܗܪ ܛܒ ܘܐܬܕܡܪ ܚܝܘܬܗ. ܘܐܝܟ ܕܠܐܒܐ ܟܫܝܪܐ ܡܫܐܠ ܗ̣ܘܐ ܠܗ ܠܗ ܟܕ ܐܡ̇ܪ. ܐܢܬ ܐܢܬ ܠܟ ܐܘܣܒܝܣ ܕܟܒܝܪ ܐܢܬ ܦܩܘܕܐ ܘܡܕܒܪܢܐ ܠܥܡܐ ܕܒܪ̈ܘܛܝܢܐ: ܗ̣ܘ ܕܝܢ ܢܫܡܬܐ ܘܡܕ̈ܥܐ ܕܐܠܗܐ. ܠܟܠܢܘܬܐ ܫܟܝܢܬܐ ܒܦܪܗܣܝܐ

ܦܢܐ ܠܗ ܦܬܓܡܐ ܒܪ ܐܡ̇ܪ. ܕܐܢܐ ܐܢܐ ܠܡ ܠܒܪܘܗܝ ܕܬܠܡ̈ܝܕܘܗܝ، ܕܡܫܝܚܐ ܐܝ ܡܢܕܡ ܢܒܝܬ. ܐܕܘܡܝܠܘܣ ܕܝܢ ܐܡ̇ܪ. ܢܒܝܢ ܒܐܝܩܘܪܗ̇ ܕܫܡܥܬܝܢ ܐܝ ܗܘ ܕܢܒܝܬ. ܠܐ ܓܝܪ ܢܒܝܢ ܫܡ ܕܒܢܝܪ ܡܢܕܡ ܡܢ ܐܘܪܝܟ ܒܡܐ ܕܡܢܝܢܢ. ܡܛܠ ܫܡܥܬܟ ܘܢܦܩܬ ܐܝܕܒܬܟ. ܐܫܪ ܒܝܪ ܫܘܠܛܢܗ ܕܐܠܗܐ ܘܢܝܫܘ ܢܐܠܗܐ ܕܠܗܠܡ. ܐܝܟ ܕܠܒܪܐ ܙܕܩܐ ܘܫܒܝܚܐ܆ ܕܢܘܕ ܒܡܕܡܢܘܗܝ، ܘܡܕܝ ܒܫܘܒܚܘܗܝ، ܦܣܩܝܢ ܒܗ. ܒܡܕܒܪܐ ܕܬܫܡܫ ܠܐܠܗܐ ܒܠ ܢܦܫ ܫܒܝܢ: ܘܒܐܝܕܝ، ܒܡܕܒܪܐ ܕܡܫܡܥܐ ܘܢܣܒܐ ܕܠܘܬ ܘܕܐܦܠܘ. ܡܪܐܝܢ ܒܡܕܒܪܬܐ ܫܕܪ ܠܝ: ܕܒܗܘܢ ܬܫܡܫ ܘܬܫܦܪ ܠܐܠܗܐ. ܘܗܐ ܕܢܬܗܡܡܝܢ ܠܝ ܬܠܝܢ. ܗܐ ܒܬܒܗ ܕܡܠܟܘܬܐ ܠܝ ܐܫܬܪܪ ܡܕܡܐܢܬ. ܐܝܟ ܪܕܝܐ ܕܐܘܫܕܢ ܘܒܡܕܒܪܐ ܕܐܠܗܐ. ܕܡܢܝܢ ܬܫܬܘܕܒ ܕܐܢܝܐ ܢܒܝܐ ܦܠܓܐ ܐܝܬ ܠܗ ܠܘܬܟ: ܘܐܘܫܦ ܘܢܗܒ. ܠܗ ܒܬܒܗ ܕܡܘܢܒܐ. ܘܦܠܠܗ ܡܢܗ ܐܝܟ ܓܒܪܐ ܕܐܕܟ ܡܢܐ ܦܢܡܐ ܗܘܐ ܠܗ ܕܢܒܕ.܀

ܦܫܡܐ ܕܝܢ ܕܒܬܒܐ ܕܐܫܬܪܪ ܠܗ ܡܢ ܦܪܘܢܐ ܐܝܬܘܗܝ، ܗܘܐ ܗܢܐ. ܡܛܠ ܕܡܢ ܢܦܪܐ ܫܘܠ ܠܡ ܢܫܢܐ ܕܪܘܝܬܟ ܘܒܡܘܫܗ ܕܐܝܕܒܬܟ. ܗܘܐ ܠܡ

ܓܒ̈ܝܢܝ. ܕܠܐ ܢܣܛܘܢ ܡܢ ܐܘܪܚܢ ܐܦܠܐ ܢܫܬܢܘܢ ܡܢ ܪܒܘܬܢ. ܐܢ ܐܝܬ ܒܟܠ ܬܕܪܘܢ ܢܦܫܢ ܘܬܒܪܝ ܘܠܘܡܝܢ. ܠܐ ܓܝܪ ܦܐܫܐ ܠܢ. ܕܠܐܢܫ̈ܐ ܫ̈ܠܝܛ ܒܐܝܕܝܗܘܢ ܘܢܗܝܪ ܒܡܣܟܠܘܬܗܘܢ. ܡܛܠ ܬܠ̈ܬܐ ܕܡܬܒܥܝܢܘܬܐ ܕܡܕܡ ܡܕܡ. ܢܚܫܘܒ ܢܦܫܐ ܐܢܘܢ ܡܕܡ: ܒܝܕ ܡܢܝܢ ܒܚܝܠܐ ܕܕܝܒܬܗܘܢ ܠܡܒܕܪܘ ܒܗܝܢ ܒܝ̈ܫܘܬܐ ܕܡܠܟܘܬܐ. ܐܘ ܒܡܘܒܪ̈ܐ ܕܢܫܝܢ ܠܥ̈ܠܡܐ. ܝܕܥܝܢ ܓܝܪ ܒܗܘܢ ܒܡܘܒܪ̈ܐ ܒܥ̈ܢܝܐ ܢܗܝܪ̈ܬܐ ܕܢܒܝܐ. ܘܐܫܟܚܝܢ ܕܢܫܬܕܪܘܢ. ܕܐܢ ܫܘܒܚܐ ܠܐ ܡܬܚܫܒ ܠܡܬܒܥ̈ܝܢܐ. ܡܠܟܘܬܐ ܠܡܬܘܡܝ ܠܐ ܡܨܝܐ. ܕܠܢ̈ܫܐ ܐܢܘܢ ܓܝܪ ܕܡܫܬܘܕܝܢ ܒܗ. ܐܢ ܗܘ ܕܗܠܝܢ ܫܒܠܝܢ ܚܢܢ ܕܢܬܒܥ. ܘܢܒܥܐ. ܐܗܡܝܢ ܕܝܢ ܡܢ ܦܠܐܬܐ. ܘܗܕܐ ܠܚܘܕ ܚܕܐ ܕܐܠܝܨܐ ܬܒܥܝܢ ܡܢ ܟܠ. ܕܐ̈ܠܗܐ ܡܢ ܗܫܐ ܢܫܬܓܪܘܢ: ܘܗ̈ܝܟܠܝܗܘܢ ܢܬܦܫܘܢ ܘܟܠܬ̈ܗܘܢ ܢܬܒܥܝܢ ܘܡܕܒܚ̈ܝܗܘܢ ܘܦܘܪ̈ܢܝܗܘܢ ܐܝܟ ܠܐ ܢܗܘܘܢ. ܚܬܝܬܐ ܒܒܪ ܠܗܝܢ. ܘܝܒ̈ܝܫܢ ܕܟܠ ܡܕܡ ܡܢ ܕܘܪܫ ܢܫܬܕܪܬ. ܐܝܟܢܐ ܕܐܝܟ ܡܢ ܢܦܫܗ ܢܦܘܫ. ܘܢܣܬܒܪ ܘܢܗܪ ܠܐ̈ܠܗܐ ܕܠܐ ܡܬܬܝܢ. ܠܐ ܓܝܪ ܦܓܥܐ ܠܐܝܕܝܥܬܐ ܗܕܐ. ܕܐܢ ܐܝܬ ܒܝܫܘܬܐ ܦܓܥܐ ܬܫܬܡܥ. ܠܦܘܡܝܢ. ܘܬܬܦܠܐ

ܟܠ ܣܓܕܬܐ ܕܐ̈ܠܗܐ. ܒܡܪܐ ܟܠܗ ܕܠܐ ܬܗܘܐ ܐܬܐ ܒܬܪܟ. ܘܡܬܬܓܪ ܐܢܬ ܒܡܫܬܡܥܢܘܬܟ ܫܢ̈ܐ ܕܒܦ̈ܬܒܘܢ܆ ܘܡܬܚܣܢܐ ܐܦ ܡܠܟܘܬܢ ܡܢ ܕܠܡܐܒܕ ܕܡܐ ܦܓܪܐ. ܠܐ ܓܝܪ ܚܒܝܢ ܒܐܒܕܢܗ ܕܐܘܣܕܝܢ ܐܦܠܐ ܕܢܦܣܘܪ ܘܢܬܒܪ ܡܛܝܒܐ ܕܢܝܠܘܬܢ܆ ܘܦܠܓ ܡܥܒܕܝܢ ܐܢܬ ܠܗ ܠܡܠܟܘܬܢ ܒܗ ܗܕܐ ܬܒܒܪ. ܐܦ ܚܝܢ ܒܚܠܦܘܗܝ ܕܗܕܐ ܦܪܨܘܦܝܢ ܚܝܢ ܕܢܦܪܩܢ ܦܠ̈ܓܘܬܐ ܦܓܪ̈ܢܝܬܐ: ܐܒܕܝܢ ܓܝܪ ܙܪܥܐ ܘܣܘܪܐ ܟܠܗܘܢ ܘܦܘܬܐ. ܘܐܚܝܕܝܢ ܡܫܥܒܕܢܐ ܘܒܪ. ܒܡܕܝܪܐ ܠܐ̈ܠܗܐ ܘܓܒܪܐ ܕܐ̈ܝܠܝܢ ܢܦ̈ܫܐ ܕܐܚܘܬܢ. ܘܬܚܒܠ ܒܪ̈ܐܐ ܕܐ̈ܠܗܐ ܘܬܬܥܒܕ ܒܫ̈ܘܬܐ ܕܡܢ ܥܠܡ. ܘܬܬܚܒܪܘܢ ܐܦ ܬܘ̈ܕܝܬܐ ܕܡܢ ܒܬܪܟ. ܘܬܐܬܐ ܠܡܘܠܕܐ ܐܠܗܝܐ. ܘܬܬܚܕܬ ܒܬܘܬܬܘܢ ܘܬܒܠܥ ܒܝܘܬܢ. ܘܕܝܬܝܪܐ ܡܢ ܟܠܗܝܢ. ܐܝܟ ܕܡܫܘܒܚܬ ܫ̈ܢܝܐ. ܒܪܐ ܕܐ̈ܠܗܐ ܕܟܠܒܘܬܐ ܬܗܘܐ. ܘܬܬܒܠ ܒܪ̈ܐܝܗ ܕܡܠܟܘܬܢ ܐܝܟ ܒܪ ܐ̈ܝܐ ܕܐ̈ܠܗܐ. ܘܐܓܒܠ ܒܐ̈ܝܪܝܟ ܟܠܗܘܢ ܓܒ̈ܐ ܕܥ̈ܕܬܐ. ܐܝܟ ܓܒܪܐ ܕܐ̈ܠܗܐ ܕܠܐ ܡܫܬܝܢ. ܘܕܢܬܗܝܡܢ ܠܟ ܟ̈ܠܗ ܘܙܪܥܢ ܠܟ ܫܘܪܝܒ. ܗܐ ܫܠܝܛܬ ܠܬܘܟ ܐܝܟ ܕܠܐܝܘܪܟ. ܒܣܪܐ ܒܡܕܝܪܐ ܡܫܝܚܐ ܕܝܘܣ ܘܕܐܦܠܘ. ܕܗܘܢ

ܢܬܠܘܢ ܒܟܬܒܐ ܐܝܠܝܢ ܕܟܬܝܒܢ ܐܬܟܬܒ ܠܗܝ. ܗܢܘܢ ܒܪ ܦܘܠܘܣ ܡܢ̈ ܚܠ ܚܠܡܝܢ. ܕ̈ܠܟܐ ܒܪ ܡܕܒܪܢܘܬܗ ܕܬܒܠ ܢܛܠܘܢ ܒܪܚܡܝܢ ܡܫܬܒܚܬܐ ܡܕܒܪܢܘܬܐ. ܕܬܒܕܪ ܢܦܫܢ ܘܬܫܒܚ ܬܫܒܚܬܐ ܒܟܢ̈ܫܗ ܕܡܠܟܘܬܢ.

ܘܡܢ ܒܬܪ ܕܐܬܡܪ، ܬܫܒܘܚܬܗ ܕܡܫܝܚܐ ܡܪܢ ܒܥܕܬܐ ܒܠܗ ܕܡܕܝܢܬܐ. ܦܩܕ ܐܣܩܘܦܐ ܘܟܠܗ ܒܡܕܪ̈ܐ ܗܘܢ ܒܐܣܛܘܟܣܐ ܕܡܕܒܪܢܘܬܗܘܢ. ܘܢܦܩܘ ܠܗ ܠܐܦܘܛܐ ܐܣܩܘܒܐ ܡܫܡܫܢܘܬܐ ܕܐܬܥܬܕ ܠܗ ܒܐܬܪ̈ܘܢܗܘܢ. ܡܢ ܢܦܠܝܢ ܫܘܦܪܐ. ܡܫܡܫܢܘܬܐ ܥܘ̈ܠܬܐ ܐܝܟ ܐܝܕܐ ܕܐܠܦܐ. ܘܡ̈ܕܝܢ ܬܫܥܝܬܐ ܕܡܕܒܪܢܘܬܐ. ܢܫ̈ܝܬܐ ܡܦܪ̈ܫܐ ܘܥܒܕ̈ܝܐ ܕܡܠܟܘܬܐ. ܘܠܠܝܐ ܕܩܘܡܐ. ܦܠܓܐ ܠܗ ܘܐܣܛܒܚܐ ܕܗܒܬ ܒܡܕܒܪܬܐ.

ܡܕܝܢܗ ܕܝܢ ܕܐܠܗܐ. ܠܐ ܚܙܪ ܒܗܝܢ ܒܡܫܡܫܢܘܬܗ ܕܠܡܕܐ. ܐܠܐ ܐܗܦܟ ܐܦܝ̈ܗ، ܡܢܗܝܢ. ܘܐܗܠ ܒܗܝܢ ܘܒܡܫܒܪ̈ܢܘܬܗܝܢ. ܘܠܒܪ ܒܗܘܢ ܒܒܡܕܒ̈ܪܝܗ ܕܢܦܠܬܐ ܒܝܕ ܐܚܪ̈ܢ. ܢܦܠܘܪ ܒܟܘܢ ܡܫܝܚܝܐ. ܘܒܐܒܘܒܘܢ ܘܦܠܓܐ. ܗ̇ܘ ܕܠܗ ܦܠܚܝܢ ܐܢܫܘܢ. ܘܠܐ ܐܡܪܘ ܠܗ ܠܥܢܝܐ ܕܥܕܪܘܢ ܕܗܘ ܘܡܫܡܫܢܘܬܗ ܒܡܢܗ ܢܐܘܠܝ ܠܐܒܝܬܐ. ܗ̇، ܕܠܘܬ ܣܘܡܘܢ ܒܪ

ܦܘܫܩܗ ܐܬܐܡܪܬ. ܡܢ ܗܘ ܫܠܝܚܐ ܕܐܠܗܐ ܪܝܫ ܬܠܡ̈ܝܕܐ. ܐܦ ܐܢܘܢ ܒܡܫܪ̈ܝܗ ܕܝܘܠܦܢܐ ܘܡ̈ܠܟܢܗ ܕܝܘܠܦܢܘܬܐ ܕܠܒܢܬܗܘܢ ܠܦ̈ܫܝܛܐ ܘܐܦܠܝܬܗܘܢ ܠܒܪ̈ܝܬܐ: ܒܝܕ ܡ̈ܠܝܗ ܕܫܘܬܦܘܬܗܘܢ. ܢܐܬܐ ܒܒܢܝܐ ܕܠܐ ܝܕܥܝܢ ܐܢܘܢ ܡܢ ܫܠܝܚܐ ܐܒܗ̈ܝܐ ܕܠܗܘܢ. ܘܒܫܒܬܐ ܕܠܐ ܡܒܪܟܝܢ ܐܢܘܢ. ܘܬܗܘܐ ܡܢܗܘܢ ܬܟܒܬܐ ܒܒܢܘܬܐ. ܘܟܪ̈ܝܗܘܢ. ܢܣܒܝܢ ܝ̈ܠܕܬܐ ܕܠܫܢܗܘܢ. ܘܢܬܦܘܢ ܘܢܬܦܪ ܦܪܘܢܐ ܕܫܪܝܪܘܢ: ܗܢܐ ܕܐܬܬܐ ܠܐܪ̈ܢܘܗܝ ܦܓܥܐ ܕܐܒܕܢܘܢ: ܐܕܘܟܣ ܕܝܢ ܗܠܝܢ ܒܢܦܫܗ ܡܬܕܡܪ ܗܘܐ ܘܡܬܟܠܐ. ܘܐܝܟ ܕܠܦܘܪܣܐ ܕܗܘܒܪܢܗ. ܒܢ̈ܝܫܬܐ ܕܒܝܠ ܡܬܢܝܚ ܗܘܐ ܒܡܗ ܒܪ ܐܡܪ. ܕܠܘ ܠܟ ܐܡܪܢܐ ܕܝܟܝܢ ܒܐܝܘܪ ܝܟܝܢ ܒܐܝܘܪ ܐܘ ܦܘܫܩ. ܘܗܕܐ ܠܟ ܒܐܝܢܘܬܐ ܗܝ ܕܐܝܬܝܕ ܫܘܠܦܗ ܕܒܠܡܐ ܦܠܓܐ ܘܒܢܐ ܕܠܒܠܟ. ܐܝܟ ܒܪ ܦܫܝܛܗ ܫܡܝܟ ܒܬ̈ܘܬܒܘܗ: ܘܒܕܝܘܪܬ ܒܠܒܗ ܫܒܘܩܬܟ: ܐܝܟ ܕܠܐܒܐ ܦܠܓܐ ܡܗܡܒܬܐ ܫܕܪ ܠܟ: ܘܐܢܬ ܒܫܘܬܦܘܬܟ ܒܡ̈ܠܐ ܕܝܟܝܢܐ ܘܕܡ̈ܝܘܬܐ ܐܝܟ ܕܒܐܒ̈ܐ ܕܟܬܒ̈ܝܗ. ܐܢܬ ܬܕܥ ܕܐܢܐ ܡܫܡܫ ܐܢܐ ܡܢ ܕܡܟ. ܒܪܡ ܕܝܢ ܐܠܝܢ ܕܐܬܦܫܩ ܠܝ ܘܠܐ ܠܗ ܕܐܫܬܠܡܐ. ܘܫܡܥ

ܚܪܒܗ ܠܓܪܘܢܐ ܘܩܪܒܗ ܠܐܘܣܒܝܣ ܒܪ ܫܡܫܓܪܐ ܘܐܡܪ ܠܗ. ܗܠܝܢ ܠܡ ܬܪܬܝܢ ܕܡܬܚܙܝܢ ܠܝ ܠܒܝܢܝ ܗܫܐ. ܐܝܟ ܬܠܬܐ. ܕܐܝܟܐ ܚܕܐ ܡܢ ܬܪܬܝܢ ܚܒܪ ܠܝ. ܐܘ ܡܫܡܫܢܘܬܗ ܕܬܠܬܐ ܘܬܫܠܡ ܠܒܝܢܗ: ܘܢܒܕܩܝܢ ܪܝܫܐ ܘܦܩܘܕܐ ܒܠ ܟܠܗܘܢ ܒܩܘܪܒܐ ܕܐܠܗܐ: ܐܝܟ ܕܐܬܝܬܝܢ ܐܦ ܗܫܐ ܪܝܫܐ ܕܟܠܗܘܢ ܐܦܣܩܘܦܐ. ܐܘ ܗܢܐ ܗܘܦܟܐ ܠܓܒܪܐ ܒܒܝܢܝܐ ܕܢܟܪܘܬܝ. ܐܦ ܗܫܐ ܚܙܝ ܗܢܐ ܦܬܓܡܐ ܡܦܝܢܐ ܐܝܬ ܠܡܠܠܐ ܕܫܠܝܚܝ ܠܘܬܝ.

ܡܕܝܢ ܕܝܢ ܕܐܠܗܐ ܚܙ ܒܢܦܫܗ ܘܐܡܪ ܠܗ ܠܐܪܘܦܠܣ. ܕܒܫܪܪܐ ܠܡ ܕܐܝܢܐ ܢܦܩ ܐܢܐ ܫܠܝܚܝ. ܕܡܠܟܐ ܩܪܐ ܐܝܬ ܠܗ ܠܥܝܢܐ ܘܠܐ ܬܘܪ ܠܓܘܢܐ. ܕܢܒܡ ܠܐܠܗܐ ܒܒܘܕܗ ܘܢܕܡ ܫܠܡܘܬܐ ܠܒܪܬܗ. ܘܢܦܠ ܫܒܝܐ ܡܢ ܫܪܪܗ. ܘܒܒܪ ܒܗܝܡܢܘܬܗ. ܘܒܒܪ ܘܐܫܬܝ ܒܣܓܪܬ ܫܐܕܐ ܘܒܦܘܠܣ ܦܬܟܪܐ ܘܡܢܝܐ ܐܝܬ ܠܝ ܕܢܐܡܪ ܡܢ ܗܫܐ. ܐܠܐ ܗܝ ܕܐܡܪ ܢܒܝܐ ܠܐܠܗܐ[1]. ܕܡܛܠܬܟ ܐܬܩܛܠܢ ܟܠܝܘܡ. ܘܐܬܚܫܒܢ ܐܝܟ ܐܡܪܐ ܠܢܟܣܬܐ. ܘܐܡܪ ܡܕܡܘܗܝ ܪܝܫܗ ܠܣܝܦܐ. ܘܢܦܩ ܦܘܪܗ ܠܣܘܦܐ ܘܐܡܪ.

1) Psalm XLIV, 22.

ܩܪܘܒ ܒܪܝ، ܘܡܫܡܠܐ ܡܢܕܡ ܕܐܬܦܩܕ ܠܟ. ܘܟܕ ܫܡܥܐ ܐܪܘܣܛܘܣ ܗܘ ܡܢܗܘܢ ܘܡܠܟܐ ܪܒܐ ܦܩܕܐ ܗܟܢܐ ܡܢܕܡ ܥܠܘܗܝ ܒܢܫܐ ܕܡܕܝܢܬܐ. ܘܠܐ ܕܐܘܠܦܟ ܦܘܪܢܣܐ. ܐܠܐ ܡܫܘܕܪ ܦܘܢܝ ܐܝܟ ܕܐܫܘܕܪܟ. ܐܝܟ ܡܐ ܕܐܦ ܗܘ ܐܘܚܕ ܫܘܠܛܢܗ ܕܥܠܡܐ ܫܕܪ ܣܗܪܝܟ ܒܟܬܝ̈ܒܬܗ. ܕܥܒܕ ܐܝܬ ܐܬܪܐ ܠܫܘܒܩܢܐ ܬܪܪܟ ܢܦܫܟ ܘܬܥܒܕ ܢܡܘܣܟ. ܘܗܐ ܟܬܒܗ ܒܐܪ̈ܥܟ. ܘܐܘܬܗ ܠܓܢܐ ܠܫܡܐ ܕܐܠܗܐ. ܘܐܬܬܠܝ ܠܗ ܟܬܒܗ ܕܫܠܝܚܘܬܗ ܘܫܕܪܗ. ܘܕܪܐ ܫܕܪܘܗܝ، ܠܐܦ̈ܝ ܪܘܚܐ. ܘܐܬܗܦܟ ܘܐܡܪ ܠܗ ܠܐܪܘܣܛܘܣ. ܕܐܝܟ ܕܐܫܬܘܕܝ ܡܪܟ ܡܢ ܟܬܒܐ ܗܢܐ ܡܕܡܢܐ ܕܒܕܪ. ܗܟܢܐ ܫܬܘܕܝ ܡܢ ܡܠܟܘܬܐ. ܘܠܐ ܢܦܠ ܘܠܐ ܢܥܒܪ ܒܐܘܚܕܢܐ ܕܪ̈ܗܘܡܝܐ. ܐܠܐ ܠܒܪ ܡܢ ܐܘܚܕܢܗܘܢ ܢܗܘܐ ܐܟܕܢܗ. ܟܠ ܕܐܡܪܬ ܘܐܫܬܒܚ ܥܠ ܐܠܗܐ ܒܒܘܪܗ. ܘܐܠܨܝ ܫܕܪܬܗ ܘܦܠܓ ܬܘܪܚܬܗ. ܒܕ ܢܦܩ ܘܫܪܪܐ ܠܗ. ܕܠܐܠܗܐ ܒܪܘܟܐ ܕܥܠ ܡܬܬܚܝܒܐ ܫܕܪܬܐ ܡܢ ܥܠܡܝܢ ܒܪ̈ܟܬܗ. ܘܕܪܫ ܫܕܪܬܗ ܠܚܐܪ̈ܐ ܘܠܪ̈ܘܚܐ. ܕܚܪ̈ܪܐ ܡܟܡܢܬܘܢ ܒܟܡܗ ܠܟܬ ܠܗܘܢ. ܕܟܕܡܟܘܬ ܩܠܝܐ ܦܘܪܐ ܠܗܘܢ ܘܫܪ̈ܝܢ: ܕܐܡܪܬ، ܕܠܗܘܢ ܕܡܢܗ ܒܥܒܬ ܐܟܬܒܗ. ܗܢܐ ܠܒܪ ܐܓܪܐ ܘܦܘܪܥܢܐ

ܡܬܦܢܝܐ ܠܗܘܢ ܠܐܝܠܝܢ ܕܒܗ ܫܪ̈ܟܐ ܦܠܝܛܝܢ ܘܡܚܠܝܢ ܀

ܘܟܕ ܫܡܥ ܗܠܝܢ ܐܪܕܘܩܣ ܘܐܝܠܝܢ ܕܥܡܗ: ܘܚܙܘ ܐܝܠܝܢ ܕܐܬܚܙܝ. ܐܬܬܢܚܘ ܒܠܒܗܘܢ ܘܐܡܪܘ ܢܬܚܫܒܘܢ. ܘܗܘܘ ܒܕܘܠܒܐ ܣܓܝܐܬܐ. ܥܠ ܕܐܬܬܠܝܘ ܒܬܪܥܐ ܕܡܠܟܘܬܐ. ܘܠܝܬܘܗܝ ܗܘܐ ܠܗ ܠܡܕܢܚܐ ܕܐܠܗܐ. ܘܠܐ ܡܟܝܢ ܗܘܐ ܕܢܟܐ ܢܒܥܘܢ ܠܗ. ܚܙܐ ܡܛܠ ܒܢܝܫܘܬܗ ܕܒܥܕܬܐ. ܘܕܬܪ̈ܬܝܢ ܕܠܐ ܐܝܬܝܗ ܗܘܐ ܦܘܪܢܣܐ ܥܠ ܡܛܠܬܗ: ܘܐܬܗܦܟܘ ܦ̈ܝܫܘܢ ܡܢ ܒܢܝܚܘܬܐ. ܘܐܬܦܢܝܘ ܠܗܘܢ ܥܠ ܩܘ̈ܪܒܢܗ ܕܡܪܕܘܬܐ. ܘܚܝܢ ܗܘܘ ܒܠܒܗܘܢ ܡܢܐܝܬ

ܒܝܘܠܝܢܘܣ ܕܝܢ ܐܪܝܐ ܕܐܝܬܘܗܝ، ܗܘܐ ܚܕ ܡܢ ܩܘ̈ܪܒܢܘܗܝ ܕܡܗܝܡܢܐ. ܐܬܝܗܒ ܒܬܓܡܐ ܠܐܪܕܘܩܣ ܟܕ ܐܡܪ. ܡܢܗ ܕܦܩܕ ܠܝ ܡܢ ܡܪ̈ܝ. ܚܘܝ ܕܢܗܒ ܒܫܝܢܗ. ܘܢܛܠ ܐܝܕܐ ܠܡܘܕܪ̈ܝ.

ܚܝ ܦܘܩܕܢܐ ܡܢܕܡ ܒܡܬܪ̈ܒܬܐ ܡܢ ܡܪ̈ܝ ܥܠ ܗܢܐ ܡܘܬܪܢܐ ܠܐ ܐܝܬܘܗܝ. ܘܠܝ ܢܬܚܫܒ ܫܡܪ ܡܢ ܚ̈ܠܒܐ ܕܗܘܘ ܡܕܒܪܝܢ. ܕܡܕܝܪ ܡܢܝ ܒܠܒܕ ܦܘܩܕܢܗ ܘܡܬܪ̈ܒܬܗ ܕܡܠܟܐ ܠܐ ܗܘܝܢ ܡܫܪ̈ܢ. ܐܪܕܘܩܣ ܐܡܪ ܐܦ ܠܗܘܢ ܕܠܒܗܘܢ ܐܝܟ ܒܟܡ ܡܬܪ̈ܒܬܐ: ܡܢ ܐܝܕܐ ܫܘܠܛܢܗ ܕܡܠܟܐ ܡܠܟܘܬܗ.

ܒܠܘܣܝܣ ܐܡܪ. ܚܕ ܡܢ ܡܬܠܘܢ ܬܫܥܝ̈ܬܗ ܕܘܠܝܬܐ ܠܐ ܦܣܩܝܢ. ܘܡܕܡ ܕܢܦܐ ܠܡܘܡܢ ܠܐ ܫܒܩܝܢ. ܕܠܡܢܐ ܗܟܝܠ ܐܝܟ ܢܣܒܪ ܟܠܡ ܡܘܬܪ̈ܬܐ. ܗܟܝܢ ܐܕܘܡܦܣ ܐܘܪܦ ܢܩܒ ܠܗ ܠܒܠܘܣܝܣ ܘܠܣܒܪ̈ܘܗܝ، ܒܬܒܗ ܕܡܣܩܒܠܐ. ܘܐܡܝܪ ܠܗܘܢ ܒܗ ܡ̈ܠܐ ܡܬܚܫ̈ܬܐ ܕܚܝܘܬܐ. ܕܠܐ ܐܝܟܐ ܠܝ ܕܒܠܗܝܢ ܢܩܒܘܢ ܐܝܟ ܒܬܒܢܝܬ ܕܠܐ ܒܠܚܘܕ ܐܝܠܝܢ ܕܚܒܝܒܝܢ ܠܗܕܪ̈ܗ ܕܒܠܬ ܒܫܘܠܡܐ ܓܝܪ ܕܒܠܗܝܢ ܡܠܘ̈ܗܝ، ܒܬܒ ܠܗܘܢ ܡܒܢܐ. ܡܛܠ ܠܡ ܕܡܫܬܡܠܝܢ ܒܟܠ ܐܢ ܒܫܒܚܬܐ ܕܐ̈ܠܗܐ ܡܗܝܡܢܐ. ܗܠܝܢ ܕܒܪ ܒܢܝܘ ܡܢܗ ܡܠܐ ܐܢܫܐ ܕܡܕܒܪܢܘܬܐ ܕܡ̈ܠܟܐ ܐܠܗ̈ܐ ܕܡܢ ܦܪܡܝܢ: ܦܪܢܣܐ ܗܘܬ ܠܡܫܝܚܐ. ܐܢܫܐ ܕܝܢ ܐܝܟ ܕܒܪ ܐܢܫܐ ܗܝܡܢܘܬܗܘܢ ܢܗܝܪܘܬܐ ܕܐ̈ܠܗܐ. ܦܕܡ ܐܒܘܗܘܢ ܕܒܝܬ ܦܘܠܦܘܣ ܗܒܬ ܢܦܫ ܢܠܦܘܢ، ܘܕܪ̈ܫܝ ܘܡܘ̈ܬܒܝ ܪܒܝܬ ܪ̈ܒܝܢܘܬܗܘܢ ܕܐ̈ܠܗܐ ܕܒܠܝܒܘܢ، ܠܐ ܓܝܪ ܦܒܢܐ ܠܝ: ܕܒܐܝܕܐ ܢܦܘܪܬܐ ܘܕܢܠܬܐ ܐܝܬܝܗܘܢ ܗܝܡܢܘܬܗܘܢ ܠܗܘܬ ܐ̈ܠܗܐ ܕܠܐ ܡܬܝܢ. ܗܢܘܢ ܕܠܐ ܗܘܐ ܗܘܐ ܒܡ̈ܠܐ ܚܢ̈ܝܦܬܐ ܘܦܪ̈ܘܣܬܐ ܡܫܬܕܪܝܢ ܗܝܡܢܘܬܐ ܕܐܢܫܐ. ܐܠܐ ܒܡ̈ܠܐ ܕܪ̈ܝܫܐ ܘܫܩ̈ܝܠܐ ܘܐ̈ܢܫܐ. ܡܛܠ ܗܢܐ ܒܪ ܢܦܫ ܐ̈ܠܗܐ ܒܡܗܝܡܢܘܬܗ

ܕܪ̈ܚܡܘܗܝ܆ ܘܐܬܩܪܒܘ ܘܫܪܝܘ ܢܫܩܘ̈ܢܘܗܝ ܠܩ̈ܠܐ ܘܐܕܪ̈ܟܘ ܣܘܟܠܗܘܢ ܕܠܘܬܗܘܢ܂ ܕܝܢ ܡܘܫܬܐ ܘܟܒܝܪ ܦܘܣܩܐ܂ ܕܫܘܐ ܗ̇ܝ ܡܢܝܢܬܗܘܢ܆ ܕܡܕܢܚ ܬܡܢܝܐ܂ ܘܬܦܪܘܩ ܒܫܡܫܘܬܐ ܕܐ̈ܠܗܝܗ̇܂ ܘܬܬܪܒ ܘܬܢܚܡ ܘܬܚܕܐ ܥܡܗ܂ ܘܬܬܒܣܡ ܒܣܘ̈ܕܪܘܗܝ܆. ܘܗܘ ܗܟܝܠ ܟܢܫܘܗܝ ܠܟܠܗ ܒܐܬܪܐ ܕܐܬܪ̈ܚܘ ܐܠܗ̈ܐ. ܘܥܒܕܘ ܠܗ ܐܝܟ ܠܐܪܣܛܘܦܘܠܝܣ ܡܕܝܢܬܗ̇ ܕܟܠܗܘܢ܂ ܘܠܡܕܡ̈ܐ ܩ̈ܕܝܫܐ ܕܒܗ̇܂ ܘܢܥܡܪܘܢ ܒܢܝܐ ܕܐܠ̈ܗܐ܆ ܘܢܫܠܡܘܢ ܬܘܕܝܬܐ ܕܐܬܪ̈ܒܘ.

ܘܟܕ ܐܬܩܪܝ܆ ܟܬܝ̈ܒܬܗ ܕܡܫܝܚܝܐ ܘܕܡ ܒܥܡܐ ܟܠܗ ܕܡܕܝܢܬܐ܂ ܡܩܕܫܘ ܫܬܝܢ ܗܘܘ ܘܕܝܢ̈ܝܢ. ܘܡܕܝܢܬܗܘܢ ܬܘܒ ܟܕ ܬܢܝܢ ܗܘܘ ܘܫܒܚܝܢ܂ ܫܘܕܥܬܐ ܠܡܘ̈ܕܝܐ ܘܠܡ̈ܟܣܢ܂ ܘܐܟܠܐ ܘܟܪܘܬܐ ܠܒܢ̈ܝܐ ܟܠܗ ܕܟܢܫܐ ܐܠܗܐ܂ ܡܫܬܥܝܢ ܗܘܘ ܕܝܢ ܐܦ ܒܘ̈ܪܟܝܗ ܕܡܕܝܢܬܐ܂ ܐܝܟܢܐ ܗܘܘ ܠܒܪ ܡܗ̈ܝܡܢܐ ܐܦ ܗܢܘܢ܆ ܘܠܐ ܢܕܥܝܢ ܗܘܘ ܡܕܡ ܕܢܥܒܕܘܢ ܡܛܠ ܟܪ̈ܝܘܬܐ ܕܠܒܗܘܢ ܕܐܬܝܕܥܝܢ ܗܘܘ܂ ܘܐܡܪܘ ܠܗ ܠܐܪܣܛܘܦܘܠܝܣ܂ ܕܢܚܘܐ ܠܢ ܒܠ ܟܬܘ̈ܒܗ ܕܡܕܝܢܬܐ ܘܡܕܡ ܚܝܝ܂ ܘܠܘ ܒܠ ܕܒܝ̈ܬܐ ܕܫ̈ܘܪܐ܂ ܐ ܡܕܡ ܦܩܕ ܠܝ ܡܪܝ܂ ܗܐ ܡܕܝܢܬܐ ܟܠܗ̇ ܘܡܕܝܢܬܟ. ܒܟܕ ܟܠ ܕܦܩܕ ܠܟ܂ ܠܝ ܠܐ ܐܪܡܐ ܠܝ ܘܠܐ

ܠܡܘܒܠ ܝܒܝܫܗ ܕܡܪܝ̈ܢ ܗܘܝܢ. ܘܠܐ ܡܢ ܐ̈ܚܝܢ ܡܬܒܬܥܝܢ ܣܝܢ. ܗܠܝܢ ܓܝܪ ܟܠܗܘܢ ܕܒܝܫܝܢ ܡܢ ܐܝܣܘܦܘܣ ܒܟܕܒܘܬܐ. ܐ̈ܚܝܢ ܐܢܘܢ ܘܣܢ̈ܝܩܝܢ. ܘܠܘ ܕܝܠܝ ܗ̣ܝ، ܕܢܟܝܢܐ ܟ̈ܠܒܬܐ. ܐܝܟܢܐ ܕܝܗܒܬ ܒ̈ܢܬܐ. ܐܡܪ ܠܗܘܢ ܐܝܣܘܦܘܣ. ܗܐ ܚܙܝܬܘܢ ܠܟܠܝܐܬ ܥܠ ܢܦܫܟܘܢ. ܕܟ̈ܠܒܐ ܪܒܝܥܝܢ ܐܢܬܘܢ ܕܐܝܣܘܦܘܣ ܘܐܠܝܢ ܕܒܒܝܬܗ. ܒܠܟܣܢܬܘܣ ܐܝܟ ܕܗܘܝܢ ܦܩܘܕܐ ܕܠܡܘܢ ܣܒܪܘܗܝ، ܐܡܪ ܠܗ. ܡܢܘ ܓܝܪ ܡܫܬܒܪܐ ܠܝ ܕܒܐܠܗܐ ܒܒܝܬ ܐܝܬ ܠܝ ܕܢܦܩܘܪ. ܐܝܣܘܦܘܣ ܐܡܪ. ܡܢܘ ܐܝܬܘܗܝ، ܒܒܘܥܐ ܕܠܐ. ܠܟܣܢܬܘܣ ܐܡܪ. ܡܫܝܚܝܐ ܕܐܬܪܘܡܦ ܥܠ ܐ̈ܦܝ ܒ̈ܢܬܗ. ܐܝܣܘܦܘܣ ܐܡܪ. ܐܢ ܒܗܢܐ ܪܒܝܢܐ ܐܝܬܝܟܘܢ. ܒܡܢܐ ܒܝܬܐ ܐܝܬ ܠܟܘܢ ܕܬܫܟܚܘܢ. ܠܟܣܢܬܘܣ ܐܡܪ. ܡܢ ܥܒܕܐ ܐܘ ܣܓܝܐ ܐܝܟ ܗܕܐ. ܕܒܕ ܡܠܟܐ ܒܥܒܠ ܠܐ ܣܓܝܐ ܠܝ: ܘܒܠ ܒܘܪܣܝܐ ܕܡܠܟܘܬܟ ܒܥܒܠ ܠܐ ܡܬܒ: ܘܫܠܛܢܗ ܒܥܒܠ ܒܠܝܢ ܠܐ ܐܡܠܟ. ܗܐ ܓܝܪ ܒ̈ܢܘܗܝ، ܘܠܒ̈ܢܘܗܝ، ܡܬܒܪܝܢ ܒܫܘܩܐ ܕܡܕܝܢܬܐ: ܣܠܩ ܗܘܦܠܝܘܣ ܘܡܗܝܡܢܘܬܐ ܕܡܠܟܐ. ܘܡܢܐ ܕܐܬܪ ܡܢ ܗܕܐ ܐܝܬ: ܐܠܐ ܕܣܠܩ ܐܬܪܐ. ܘܠܐ ܢܣܠܩ ܫܪܪܗ ܕܐܠܗܘܢ: ܘܕܝܢܘܬܐ ܢܒܪ̈ܝܐ ܠܐܘܚܕܢܐ ܒܠܗ

ܕܪ̈ܗܘܡܝܐ ܘܠܐ ܢܬܒܥܐ ܠܡܫܝܚܘܬܐ ܕܐܬܠܒܫܘ ܠܝ ܐܩ̈ܢܘܡܝܢ. ܠܡܬܘܪ ܕܝܢ ܘܠܡܬܕܪܫܘ. ܕܟܕ ܡܬܟܪܝܢ ܒܕܒܝܠ ܒܐܬܘ̈ܬܐ ܚ̈ܠܝܦܢ. ܠܓܒܐ ܕܫܒܩܘܬܗ ܘܕܡܟܗ ܠܐܬܘ̈ܬܐ ܒܟܠܗܘܢ ܕܐܘܫܥܝܢ. ܐܬܪ̈ ܠܗܘܢ ܐܪܘܣܛܘ. ܕܗܝܢ ܗܟܢܐ ܕܗܢܐ ܐܝܬܘܗܝ ܟܢܫܘ̈ܢ. ܐܬܠ ܐܢܫܐ ܠܝ ܠܘܬ ܡ̈ܠܟܐ ܕܫܕܪܘ. ܘܗܘ ܐܝܟ ܕܡܟ ܢܟܒ ܒܟܒܘܢ ܫܘܒܚܐ ܕܗܝܟܢܘܬܗܘܢ. ܡܗ̈ܝܡܢܐ ܕܝܢ ܕܐܬܒܫܘ ܗܘܘ ܠܡܫܝܚܘܬܗ ܕܗܢܐ ܘܡܟܪܙܝܢ. ܐܪܝܟܘ ܒܠ ܪܘ̈ܟܒܝܗ ܕܪܗܘܡܝ̈ܐ ܘܐܡܪܝܢ. ܟܕ ܕܐܫܬܐ ܪ̈ܚܝܡܘ ܒܕܘܠܬܐ ܕܐܝܟܝܢܐ. ܐܝܟܢ ܐܢܬܘܢ ܕܐܬܝܬܘܢ ܒܠܝܢ ܒܟܫܬܐ. ܘܒܠܠܬܘܢ ܬܘܪܒ ܡܕܒܫܬ̈ܐ ܒܕܠܐ ܐܝܟܢ ܐܢܬܘܢ ܠܡܫܡܥܘ ܐܝܟܢܐ ܕܡܠܟܐ. ܗܕܐ ܕܝܢ ܬܘܗܐ ܫܪܝܪܐ ܠܟܘܢ. ܕܐܝܟܢܐ ܕܡܠܟܐ ܡܬܘܡܝܡ ܐܦ ܒܟܕ ܠܐ ܬܐܝܟܢܘܢ. ܡܟܝܠ ܕܝܢ ܐܝܕܐ ܠܐܝܟܢܐ ܕܡܠܟܐ ܘܡܬܘܡܝܡ. ܒܗܠܝܢ ܕ̈ܝܢܬ ܩ̈ܠܐ ܡܬܚܫܫܝܢ ܗܘܘ ܡܗ̈ܝܡܢܐ ܒܠܐܝܬ. ܘܕܡ ܒܗܠܝܢ ܒܟܠܐ ܕܪܗܘܡܝ̈ܐ. ܘܢܩܫܝܢ ܗܘܘ ܒܟܦ̈ ܘܪ̈ܦܣܝܢ[1]) ܘܡܙܝܢܝܢ. ܘܡܬܠܒܛܝܢ ܗܘܘ ܘܡܣܬܒܛܝܢ ܠܢܦܫܐ ܥܠ ܒܢܝ̈ܢ ܕܒܠܬܐ. ܘܢܦܩܘܗܝ ܠܐܪܘܣܛܘܣ ܡܗ̈ܝܡܢܐ ܘܢܦ̈ܩܘ. ܐܝܟ ܬܠܬܐ ܐ̈ܠܦܝܢ

1) Ezekiel VI, 11

ܠܒ̈ܢܝܢ. ܘܐܡܪܝܢ ܕܐܝܢ ܠܐ ܡܥܒܕܝܢ ܚܢܢ ܐܝܢܐ ܠܡܫܝܚܗ ܕܡܠܟܐ. ܘܬܬܒܥܐ ܠܗ ܚܠܦܬܐ ܠܫ̈ܠܝܚܐ ܥܠ ܬ̈ܪܒܝܬܗ ܕܡܫܝܚܘܬܐ ܘܕܡܫܡܠܝܘܬܐ. ܕܡܫܝܚܘܬ ܢܦ̈ܫܐ ܕܐܠ̈ܗܐ ܘܒܥܒܪܬ ܫ̈ܠܝܚܘܗܝ܇ ܘܡܫܬܪܬ ܘܐܫܬܒܩܬ ܒܝܬ ܢܒ̈ܝܐ: ܘܐܘܕܝܬ ܒܝܬ ܡܘ̈ܫܬ܀ ܘܐܡܪܬ، ܗܘ ܒܗ ܡܘܡܐ ܕܢܫܝܐ ܠܢܦ̈ܫܬܗ ܒܕ ܡܫܬܬܪܝܢ: ܘܢܗܠ ܒܗ ܐܝܟ ܕܐܘܠܗ ܒܗ ܐܠܗܝܢ. ܒܢܒ̈ܝ ܕܒܝܬ ܕܘܠܦܢܐ ܘܡܫܡܫܢܐ ܡ̈ܠܟܐ ܡܫ̈ܒܚܐ: ܕܬܫܘ ܢܦ̈ܫܗ ܕܡܐ ܘܦܠܚܘ ܫܬ̈ܝܐ ܕܫܝܪܬܗ.

ܒܕ ܕܝܢ ܐܬܐ ܦܘܠܘܣ ܐܘܣܒܝܘܣ ܒܗܠܝܢ. ܫܠܚ ܠܗ ܠܐܕܘܦܘܣ. ܕܠܐ ܠܝ ܘܠܬܫܡܫܬܗ ܕܒܝܬܐ ܕܡܦܪܬܗ ܗܝ ܕܐܬܦܠܓܬ ܠܝ. ܠܒܟܐ ܗܝ ܠܝ ܠܒܪ ܕܐܡܪܬ ܡܦܠܓܬܗ. ܘܠܐ ܢܕܘܫ ܠܘܚܡܐ. ܘܐ ܗܘܕܝܐ ܒܥܠܕܒܒܝܢ ܡܦܪܫܢ ܠܝ ܓܝ. ܕܒ ܘܫܪ ܡܠܟܐ ܒܟܪ ܐܢܬ. ܒܡܟܐ ܠܒܪ ܥܠܗ ܕܐܢܬ ܒܥܒ. ܥܬܕܝܢ ܐܢܘܢ ܘܡܦܠܓܝܢ. ܘܡܫܡܥܝܢ ܐܦ̈ܝܗܘܢ ܕܢܫܕܒܘܢ ܘܕܢܬܚܪܒܘܢ܀

ܒܕ ܕܝܢ ܫܡܥ ܐܕܘܦܘܣ ܗܠܝܢ. ܩܪܐ ܠܝܗܘܕܝܐ ܘܠܫ̈ܠܝܚܐ ܘܐܡܪ ܬ̈ܪܒܐ ܒܕܪܐ ܕܒܝܬܐ. ܘܐܬܬܚܡܢܘܢ ܥܠܝܗܘܢ ܡܢ ܟܠ ܠܒܢ̈ܝܢ. ܘܐܬܬܚܡܢܘܢ ܒܡܫܘܚܬܐ

ܐܘܣܒܝܣ ܘܐܝܠܝܢ ܕܥܡܗ ܡܫܡ̈ܫܢܐ ܬܪ̈ܝܢ. ܘܫܪܝܘ ܡܪ̈ܕܐ ܘܢܦܩܘ ܠܡܕܒܪܐ ܓܠܝܬܐ. ܘܟܕ ܚܙܘ ܕܘܒܪ̈ܝܗ ܕܡܕܝܢܬܐ: ܕܐܬܬܣܝܡܘ ܒܡܫܡܫܢܐ ܐܘܣܒܝܣ ܐܦܝܣܩܘܦܐ ܘܠܘܬܗ ܒܠܗ ܕܡܕܝܢܬܐ: ܥܡ ܐܬܪܐ ܡܗܝ̈ܡܢܐ ܕܒܥܡܐ ܘܥܡܗܘܢ݁: ܘܐܝܠܝܢ ܐܦܝܣܩܘܦܐ ܕܐܬܘ ܒܝܬ ܣܗ̈ܕܐ ܠܫܢܝܩܐ. ܕܥܡܐ ܕܐܬܟܢܫܬ ܠܘܬܗ ܘܐܬܦܢܝܘ ܕܢܝܚܐ: ܢܬܦܬܚܘܢ ܬܪ̈ܥܝܗ ܕܡܕܝܢܬܐ. ܘܢܥܠܘܢ ܟܠܗܘܢ ܒܦܘ̈ܩܕܐ ܕܠܐ ܦܘܪܣܗ ܕܐܘܪܘܛܦܣ ܘܢܫܪܘܢ ܐܢܘܢ݁: ܒܚܪܬ ܠܗܘܢ ܟܠ ܠܬܪ̈ܥܝܗ ܕܪ̈ܗܘܡܝܐ. ܘܚܘܬ ܠܗܘܢ ܒܕܡܐ ܠܦܫܐ ܕܠܐ ܝܕܥܝܢ ܗܘܘ ܡܢܐ ܢܥܒܕܘܢ݁: ܕܕܚܠܝܢ ܗܘܘ ܡܢ ܝܒ̈ܘܬܐ ܕܦܠܚܘܗܝ ܕܐܚܝܕܝܢ ܗܘܘ. ܘܕܠܐ ܡܢܝܢ ܗܘܘ ܕܢܦܠܓܘܢ ܥܠ ܢܦܫܗܘܢ݂. ܒܬܪ ܕܝܢ ܒܐܪܙ. ܘܐܘܕܥܘ ܠܐܒܝܣܩܘܦܐ ܕܕܝܪ̈ܬܐ ܗܠܝܢ. ܘܫܠܚܘ ܠܗܘܢ݂. ܕܐܙܕܪܙܘ ܒܥܓܠ ܠܐܘܪܚܗܘܢ ܕܒܥܕܢܬܐ ܕܠܐ ܫܠܛܐ ܒܗܘܢ ܚܪܒܐ ܕܪ̈ܕܘܦܐ. ܒܥܕܢܐ ܓܝܪ ܕܫܢ̈ܩܐ ܘܕܡܫܕ̈ܪܢܐ ܕܐܬܬܣܝܡܘ ܥܠܝܗܘܢ݁: ܘܐܚܝܕܘ ܬܪ̈ܥܝܗ ܒܪ̈ܝܐ ܕܡܕܝܢܬܐ. ܘܗܫܐ ܐܢܘܢ݂ ܒܡܫܡܫܢܐ: ܠܐܘܣܒܝܣ ܐܦܝܣܩܘܦܐ ܘܠܐܝܠܝܢ ܕܥܡܗ̇. ܟܕ ܡܬܒܥܝܢܐ ܥܠܬܐ ܠܗܘܢ ܘܠܐܦܠܘ݂ ܥܠ ܬܪ̈ܥܝܗ ܕܡܕܝܢܬܐ. ܘܗܡܢܐ ܬܘܒ, ܒܝܬ ܣܗ̈ܕܐ

ܠܫ̈ܒܒܐ. ܕܗܒܐ ܕܐܬܝܗܒܬ ܒܠܬܐ ܘܡܠܟܘ ܕܒܫ̈ܢܝ. ܢܬܦܬܚܘܢ ܬܪ̈ܥܝܗ ܕܡܕܝܢܬܐ. ܘܡܠܟܘܢ ܟܠܗܘܢ ܡܢ ܩܛܝܪ ܕܠܐ ܦܘܪܫܢܐ ܘܢܫܪܒܘܢ ܐܢܘܢ. ܗܫܐ ܐܙܕܪܒܘ ܐܢܘܢ ܒܕܠܐ ܫܠܝܐ ܠܐ ܒܗܘܢ ܫܪܒܐ ܕܘܩܦܐ. ܫܢܝ ܓܝܪ ܠܗ ܡܠܟܐ ܕܢܘܕܥ ܢܦܩ ܓܠܝܐܝܬ. ܡܛܠ ܫܘܠܛܢܐ ܕܡܠܟܐ ܕܐܫܬܕܪ.

ܘܟܕ ܝܠܦ ܐܬܦܪܣܘ ܒܗܠܝܢ. ܓܒܪܐ ܘܢܫ̈ܐ ܫܡܥܐܝܬ ܒܪ ܐܡܪ. ܘܗ̇ ܠܡ ܕܫ̈ܠܝܡܝܢ ܐܬܟܠܘ ܟܠܗ ܡ̈ܠܟܐ ܪ̈ܘܫܐ. ܘܗܘܐ ܗܘܐ ܡܬܦܪܣܢܐܝܬ ܒܟܠܗܝܢ ܫܒ̈ܝܢܐ. ܘܐܫܬܡܥ ܠܟܠܗܘܢ ܕܡ̈ܬܐ ܕܬܡܢ. ܘܒܬܪ ܠܟܠܗܘܢ ܕܡ̈ܬܐ ܕܐܝܬ ܒܪܘܗܡܐ ܘܒܫ̈ܪܟܗ. ܟܠ ܕܡܟܝܐ ܒܫܠܡܐ ܠܡܐܪܒ ܩܘܪܝܐ. ܐܝܟ ܐܠܦ ܘܐܬܒܟܝܢܐ ܒܒ̈ܢܝܢ. ܘܗܘܘ ܟܠܗܘܢ ܫܕܐ ܢܦܫ ܘܫܪ ܪܒܝܢ. ܘܐܪܝܡܘ ܩܠܗܘܢ ܘܒܟܘ ܟܠ ܡܘܒܟܘܗ̇ ܕܡܕܝܢܬܐ. ܘܟܠ ܫܒܘܩܐ ܕܐܢ̈ܫܘܗܝ ܘܗܘܒܘ ܡܟܝܢܐ ܠܫ̈ܒܒܐ. ܠܡܟܝܟܬ ܟܠ ܚ̈ܕܝ ܐܢ̈ܫܘܗܝ ܕܡܕܝܢܬܐ. ܘܢܦܠܘ ܘܒܟܘ ܠܫ̈ܒܒܐ ܘܒܟܘ ܒܘܟܝܐ ܘܓܢܝܒܘܬܐ. ܘܟܠܗ ܗܘܬ ܠܪܘܡܝܐ ܒܠܒܝܒܘܬܐ ܪܟܝܬܐ ܒܪ ܡܫܝܚܝ ܘܡܫܠܝܢ ܫܦܝܪܐ. ܫܠܝܦܝܢ ܗܘܘ ܕܝܢ ܒܡܚܝܢ ܡܢ. ܐܦ ܐܢ̈ܫܐ ܪ̈ܘܗܡܝܐ ܐܝܟ ܡܫܒܫܒܐܝܬ ܒܒ̈ܢܝܢ. ܘܐܬܟܢܫܘܢ ܗܘܘ ܡܢ ܐܬܪ̈ܐ

ܕܒܝܬ ܢܗܪ̈ܝܢ ܕܗܘܢ ܗܠܝܢ ܕܠܒܝܫܐ ܕܐܠܗܘܬܐ: ܥܠܝܗ ܗܘܘ ܐܣܟܡܗܘܢ ܠܐܣܟܝܡܐ ܕܕܝܪ̈ܐ. ܘܦܪܣܘ ܣܕܪܗܘܢ ܘܟܠܗ ܒܝܬܗܘܢ ܠܪܗܒܘܬܐ. ܟܕ ܡܕܝܢܝܢ. ܟܕ ܐܝܟ ܠܓܒܪ ܠܐ ܡܫܬܘܕܥ ܗ̇ܘܐ ܠܗܘܢ܆ ܘܐܬܬܝܕܥܬ ܥܠܘܗ̇ܝ ܡܕܝܢܬܐ ܡܢ ܡܕܒܪܢܘܬܗܘܢ܆ ܘܬܪ̈ܝܢ ܠܡܥܠ ܒܝܬܐ. ܟܕ ܕܝܠܗܘܢ ܕܡܬܟܢܫܝܢ ܥܠܬܐ. ܘܟܕ ܚܙܘ ܐܢܘܢ ܫܡܥܐ ܘܬܗܘܪܐ. ܥܪܩܘ ܡܬܪܗܒܝܢ ܡܢ ܡܕܝܢܬܗܘܢ܆ ܡܣܬܪܝܐ ܠܒܪ ܐܪܥܐ ܕܝܠܬܐ ܘܥܒܕܬܐ ܥܠ ܡܗܘܕܝܢܐ ܘܫܡܥܐ. ܘܥܪܩܘ ܠܡܕܒܪܐ ܡܢ ܩܕܡ ܕܕܝܪ̈ܐ ܠܟܠ ܚܕ̈ܝܢ: ܘܥܠܘ ܒܗܘܢ ܒܣܘܦܪ̈ܐ ܒܝܬ ܥܘ̈ܡܐ. ܘܚܙܘ ܐܢܘܢ ܐܝܟ ܩ̈ܠܝܐ. ܘܗܘܬ ܒܗܘܢ ܢܗܪܐ ܡܢ ܢܘܗܪ̈ܐ ܘܫܦܝܪܐ ܒܟܢܐ ܫܟܝܢܐ. ܘܠܐ ܐܫܬܘܫܘ ܒܢܝܢܗܘܢ ܐܠܐ ܐܢ ܕܠܝܠܝܐ ܘܠܠ܆ ܕܗܘܬܘ ܢܦܫܗܘܢ ܒܚܫ̈ܝܫܬܐ ܘܒܫܘܠܡܐ܆ ܘܒܐܣܟܡ̈ܝܗܘܢ ܕܡܕܒܪܢܘܬܐ ܘܐܫܬܘܕܥܘ. ܘܡܢ ܒܬܪܐ ܕܕܝܪ̈ܐ ܠܐ ܐܬܝܢ ܐܦܠܐ ܚܕ. ܡܪܢܐ ܚܢܢ ܐܝܟ ܐܝܢܐ ܕܠܗܘܢ ܘܢܦܩ ܐܢܘܢ܆

ܐܕܘܩܣ ܕܝܢ ܟܕ ܚܙܐ ܕܥܪܩܬ ܚܪܒܐ ܒܡܗܘܕܝܐ. ܐܡܪ ܠܒܝܬܪܐ ܗܠܝܢ ܕܐܝܬ ܗܘܘ ܒܗܘܢ. ܠܐܝܟܐ ܕܡܫܟܚܝܢ ܐܢܘܢ ܫܕܪܘ ܢܦܫܘܢ܆ ܘܗܘ ܪܕܐ. ܘܗܘ ܗܢܘܢ ܘܐܬܦܠܓ ܒܢܦܫܗ. ܘܟܕ ܚܙܘ ܒܡܕܒܪܐ

ܗܠܝܢ ܕܟܬܒ ܐܢܘܢ ܐܕܘܡܦܣ ܘܒܪܗ. ܢܦܠܬ ܒܠܒܗܘܢ ܕܫܠܝܬܐ ܘܐܘܒܠܬܐ. ܘܡܬܒܪܟܝܢ ܗܘܘ ܘܒܟܝܢ ܐܝܟܐ ܢܣܬܪܘܢ ܢܦܫܗܘܢ ܘܐܬܟܢܫܘ ܒܝܬ ܓܠܝܐ ܚܕ. ܪܒܐ ܕܦܪܫ ܗܘܐ ܡܢ ܡܕܝܢܬܐ ܩ̈ܠܝܟܐ ܬܐܪܝܢ. ܘܣܦܩ ܠܗ ܘܣܬܪܘ ܢܦܫܗܘܢ ܡܠܟܐ ܒܕܒܪܐ: ܟܕ ܢܦܠ ܠܗܘܢ ܦܠܓܐ ܕܒܢܘܢ ܡܢ ܬܡܢ. ܘܟܕ ܢܦܩܬ ܚܪܒܐ ܘܗܘܐ ܫܠܝܐ: ܘܠܐ ܐܫܬܚܪ ܝܗܘܕܝܐ ܐܘ ܚܢܦܐ ܕܡܬܚܙܝܐ ܒܟܠܗ ܡܕܝܢܬܐ ܓܠܐܝܬ. ܐܡܪ ܠܗܘܢ ܐܕܘܒܣܘܣ ܠܕܝܪ̈ܐ ܫܒܝܪ̈ܘܗܝ. ܗܫܐ ܕܐܚܝܢ ܠܢ ܡܫܝܚܐ: ܘܚܝ̈ܝ ܚܒܝ̈ܫܝܢ ܒܒܥܠܕܒ̈ܒܝܗ ܕܕܝܪܬܐ ܘܟܘܡܪ̈ܘܗܝ ܕܓܠܝܕܐ. ܢܦܬܚ ܬܪ̈ܥܝܗ ܕܕܝܪܬܐ. ܘܢܒܐܘܗܝ ܠܙܒܢܐ ܒܙܒܢܐ ܘܠܡܥܪ̈ܒܬܗ. ܘܦܬܚܘ ܬܪ̈ܥܝܗ ܕܕܝܪܬܐ. ܘܟܠܗ ܥܡܐ ܫܠܡܐ ܠܐܘܣܒܝܣ ܐܦܝܣܩܘܦܐ ܘܠܐܝܠܝܢ ܕܥܡܗ. ܘܗܘܬ ܚܕܘܬܐ ܒܟܠܗ ܡܕܝܢܬܐ. ܒܦܘܪܩܢܐ ܕܥܒܕ ܐܠܗܐ ܠܕܝܪܬܗ. ܗܘܬ ܗܘܬ ܕܝܢ ܒܥܕܬܐ ܒܝܬ ܐܝܬܒܝ. ܕܡܢ ܟܕ ܗܘܐ ܡܢ ܗܠܝܢ ܒܡܕܝ̈ܢܬܐ ܕܢܦܠܬܐ. ܘܟܕ ܐܬܒܢܝܬ ܒܥܕܬܐ ܕܟܢ̈ܝܫܘܗܝ: ܐܦ ܐܬܚܕܬ ܕܠܐ ܡܕܝܢܬܘ ܚܕ ܡܢ ܗܠܝܢ ܒܡܕܝ̈ܢܬܐ. ܡܬܒܥܝܢ ܗܘܘ ܠܗ ܠܦܘܠܚܢܐ ܐܘܣܒܝܣ ܕܢܦܘܫ ܠܗܘܢ ܕܢܦܩܘܢ ܒܥܒܕܘܗܝ: ܐܡܪ ܠܗܘܢ ܘܪܝܫܗ ܕܐܠܗܐ. ܫܒܘܩܘ ܠܝ ܡܛܘ̈ܬܐ

ܘܫܒܩ ܡܢ̈ ܕܐܡܝܪ ܗܝ. ܡܩ̈ܒܪܝܢ ܡܝ̈ܬܘܗܘܢ[1] ܢܐܦ ܕܐܠܗܘܢ. ܘܗܢܘܢ ܕܫܪ̈ܝܐ ܠܗܕܐ ܬܠܡܝܕܘܬܐ ܪܘܚܢܝܬܐ ܕܦܠܚܬ ܒܗ. ܘܠܐ ܒܠܚܘܕ ܦܪܝܢ ܢܗܘܐ ܡܫܡ̈ܫܢܐ ܠܐܠܗܘܢ: ܘܢܫܬܒܚ ܠܗ ܕܟܠ ܢܦܫ ܒܬܫܢܝܩ.

ܒܗ ܒܝܘܡܐ ܗܢܐ. ܟܠܗ ܒܥܘܡܪܗ ܕܡܫܡܫܬܐ ܪܘܪܒܝܢܗ ܕܪܗܘܡܐ. ܐܪܥܐ ܝܕ̈ܝܥܐ ܘܡܫܬܡܗܐ: ܡܕܝܢܬܐ ܘܦܘܩܕܢܗ ܕܡܠܟܘܬܐ. ܘܒܒܝܬܗ ܬܠܬܝ ܘܫܘܒܚ ܡܠܟ̈ܘܬܐ. ܕܢܗܘܘܢ ܚܕܐ ܢܦܫ ܘܚܕ ܪܥܝܢ. ܘܢܫܬܐܠܘܢ ܡܢ ܡܕܒܪܢܘܬܐ ܕܡܕܝܢܬܐ. ܘܡܢ ܝܡܝܢܬܐ ܕܦܠܚܝܢ ܕܐܚܝܕܝܢ ܗܘܘ. ܘܒܚܝܕܐ ܐܘܝܘܬܐ ܘܒܚܝܕܐ ܫܠܡܘܬܐ. ܘܒܚܕ ܚܘܒܐ ܫܦܝܐ ܕܠܐ ܢܟܠܐ[2]: ܕܟܕ ܟܠܐ ܢܗܘܘܢ ܟܠ ܢܦܫܗܘܢ ܡܕܡ ܦܘܪܢܐ ܕܡܫܦ̈ܠܢܐ ܐܝܟ ܕܠܐ ܢܬܒܥܘܢ ܡܢ ܫܘܦܠܗ ܐܦܠܐ ܡܢ ܒܢ̈ܝܐ ܕܠܘܚܡ̈ܝܗܘܢ ܢܬܪܗܒܘܢ ܐܘ ܢܬܬܢܝܚܘܢ: ܘܐܢ ܢܚܙܝ ܟܠܗܘܢ ܦܬܓܡܐ ܕܡܦܘܪܫܐ. ܦܫܘܡ ܒܢܦܫܗܘܢ: ܘܟܠܗ ܟܠܗܘܢ ܫܪ̈ܝܐ ܘܡܫܬܠܡܢܐ.

ܘܟܕ ܠܟ ܦܘܠܚܢܐ ܐܘܟܝܬ: ܕܐܝܕܐ ܕܦܠܚܘܬܐ ܗܘܬ ܠܗܘܢ ܠܪܘܪܒܝܢܗ ܕܪܗܘܡܐ: ܕܠܐ ܬܬܦܪܣ

---

1) Matthew VIII, 22.

2) 2 Corinthians VI, 6.

ܗܝܡܢܘܬܗ̇ ܬܪܝܨܬܐ ܕܒܪܝܬܐ: ܘܕܚܠܬܗ ܘܫܘܒܚܐ ܕܢܦܫܗܘܢ ܠܡܠܟܘܬܐ ܥܠ ܟ̈ܦܐ ܫܪܪܗ ܕܐܠܗܘܗܝ. ܫܪܐ ܗܘܐ ܘܪܘܪ ܪܚܝܡܘ ܟܠܝܠܗ̇ ܕܡܫܝܚܝܘܬܗܘܢ: ܘܫܪܪܗ ܕܪܚܝܡܘܗܝ: ܘܠܐ ܡܐܢܬ ܠܗ ܠܗܢܐ ܣܒܐ ܡܒܪܟܐ ܘܡܣܟܢܐ ܐܠܗܝܐ ܕܗܢܐ ܗܘܐ. ܡܛ ܐܙܠ ܠܘܬܗܘܢ ܟܕ ܕܟܢܝܫܝܢ ܗܘܘ. ܘܝܗܒ ܠܗܘܢ ܫܠܡܐ. ܘܡܠܟܐ ܠܟܠܗܘܢ ܘܒܪܟ ܐܢܘܢ: ܘܬܫܒܘ̈ܚܬܐ ܣܓܝ̈ܐܬܐ ܕܡܢ ܟܬܒܐ ܡܠܒܒ. ܗܘܐ ܠܗܘܢ ܘܡܫܐܠ ܪܚܝܡܘܗܝ: ܟܕ ܝܗܒ ܠܗܘܢ ܫܠܡܐ ܘܡܟܠܠ ܠܡܫܝܚܝܘܬܗܘܢ: ܘܟܕ ܒܝܘܡܐ ܡܥܝܠ ܦܨܝ ܗܘܐ ܕܢܐܙܠ ܐܢܫ ܐܢܫ ܠܒܝܬܗ. ܘܢܒܘ ܣܓܕܘ ܠܗ ܘܐܬܒܪܟܘ ܡܢܗ.

ܘܟܕ ܒܪܟ ܐܢܘܢ: ܫܪܐ ܐܢܘܢ ܕܢܐܙܠܘܢ ܐܢܫ ܐܢܫ ܠܒܝܬܗ ܒܫܠܡܐ. ܘܗܘ ܗܦܟ ܠܕܝܪܗ. ܟܕ ܫܪܐ ܘܡܫܒܚ ܘܡܫܟܚ ܠܐܠܗܐ. ܘܠܦ ܕܝܢ ܝܘܠܝܢܘܣ ܒܟܠܗܘܢ ܕܝܘ̈ܡܐ ܒܪܗܘܡܝ. ܘܠܝܫܘܥ ܗܘܐ ܠܗܘܢ ܠܒܢ̈ܝ ܪܗܘܡܝ ܟܠ. ܘܡܠܟܐ ܗܘܐ ܒܠܝܗܘܢ ܚܡܬܐ ܘܪܘܓܙܐ. ܘܡܣܬܪܩ ܗܘܐ ܐܦ̈ܘܗܝ ܠܐܒܕܢܘܗܝ: ܘܕܢܟܒ ܡܢܗܘܢ ܬܘܒܬܐ ܕܝܗܒܢܘܗܝ ܕܡܬܪܥܘܗܝ. ܘܣܦ ܕܝܢ ܕܢܥܡ ܬܪܒܝܬܗ ܕܦܪܘܣܐ.

ܟܕ ܫܡܥ ܘܦܠܓܐ ܠܐܣܦܠܝܣ. ܥܒܪ ܡܕܡܘܗܝ, ܡܣܒ̈ܪܢܐ ܠܪܗܘܡܝܐ: ܕܢܣܒܪܘܢ ܗܘܘ ܥܠ

ܒܐܝܬܝܗ̇. ܘܐܫܬܠܛܬ ܥܠܝܗ̇ ܡܕܝܢܬܐ ܘܐܬܪܗܒܬ. ܘܪ̈ܘܪܒܢܝܗ̇ ܕܝܢ ܕܪ̈ܗܘܡܝܐ: ܗܠܝܢ ܕܥܠܘ ܒܡܫܟܢܐ ܕܡܫ̈ܡܫܬܐ. ܠܐ ܐܬܪܗܒܘ ܗܟܢ ܐܘ ܐܫܬܠܛܘ. ܐܠܐ ܟܕ ܝܠܦ. ܥܠ ܦܘܪܥܢܐ ܕܘܪܒ. ܠܡܐܬܐ. ܘܟܕ ܫܡܥܘ ܡܦܩܬܗ ܕܥܠܡܐ. ܘܪܘܚܐ ܕܩܘܕܫܐ. ܘܦܪ̈ܫܘ ܢ̈ܦܫܬܗܘܢ ܥܒܕ. ܘܫܕܪܘ ܠܡܩ̈ܒܠܢܐ ܘܠܫܝܢܘܬܐ ܘܐܦ ܠܝܬ̈ܡܐ. ܘܠܐܪ̈ܡܠܬܐ ܘܦܪܢܣܘ ܠܐ ܢܒܘܪ. ܐܢ̈ܫܐ ܗܘܘ ܓܝܪ ܡܪ̈ܝ ܢ̈ܦܫܬܐ. ܘܫܘܒܩܢܐ ܕܚ̈ܛܗܝܗܘܢ ܘܡܫܡܫ ܕܢܦܩ ܗܘܘ. ܐܓܠܘܗܝ ܠܒ̈ܢܝ ܒܝܬܗܘܢ. ܘܐܫܬܡܫܘ ܡܫ̈ܡܫܢܐ ܘܩܫ̈ܝܫܐ ܥܠ ܐܦܝܣܩܘܦܐ ܕܝܠܗܘܢ ܕܠܟܠ ܘܕܒܪܘ. ܘܡܕܒܪܢܐ ܕܢܐܬܐ ܦܘܪܥܢܐ ܠܡ̈ܕܝܢܬܗܘܢ. ܘܥܒܕܘ ܒܝܬܗܘܢ ܘܐܬܒܢܝܘ ܠܡܫܪ̈ܝܗܘܢ: ܘܒܬܪܗ ܕܐܠܗܐ ܒܥ ܦܘܪܥܢܐ ܐܘܣܒܝܣ ܗܘܐ ܗܘܐ ܡܕܒܪܢܗܘܢ. ܒܕܡܐ ܠܡܫܠܡܐ ܕܟܠ ܦܘܪܥܢܐ ܠܡܕܒܪܢܘܬܗܘܢ: ܘܫܕܪ ܢܒܫ ܐܢܘܢ ܒܝܬ ܐܣܝܪ̈ܐ. ܗܘܬ ܗܘܬ ܕܝܢ ܡܫܠܡܬܗ ܕܠܝܣܢܝܘܣ ܠܪ̈ܗܘܡܝܐ. ܒܐܝܪܚ ܐܕܪ ܕܫܢܬ ܫܬ ܡܐܐ ܘܥܣܪܝܢ ܘܬܠܬ ܕܡܠܟܘܬܐ ܕܝܘ̈ܢܝܐ ܒܫܢܬܐ ܘܒܫܢܝܢ ܕܗ ܒܪܘܢܐ. ܟܕ ܡܠܘ ܠܡܘܬܗ ܕܩܘܣܛܢܛܝܢܘܣ ܢ̈ܘܚܐ ܫܡ̈ܫܐ. ܒܗ ܒܝܘܡܐ ܗܢܐ ܥܠ ܦܘܪܥܢܐ ܠܪ̈ܗܘܡܝܐ. ܒܝܘܡܐ ܪܒܐ ܕܩܝܡܬܗ. ܘܒܬܘܩܦܐ

ܘܡܫܝܚܐ ܕܡܫܪܝܬܗ . ܘܡܣܘܓܐܐ ܕܠܓܒ̈ܘܪܐ ܘܡܣܘܪ̈ܢܐ ܕܠܒ̈ܢܐ .

ܘܟܕ ܒܢܝܬ ܠܗ̇ ܡܕܝܢܬܐ ܐܝܟ ܦܘܩܕܢܗ ܕܡܠܟܐ . ܘܐܬܡܠܝܬ ܒܗ̇ ܢ̈ܘܢܐ ܣܦܐ ܒܡܣܦܐ . ܠܒܪ ܠܗܠܝܢܘܢ ܠܒ̈ܢܝܐ ܕܡܠܟܘܬܐ̣ . ܘܫܠܡ ܕܝܬܒ ܥܠ ܡܠܟܘܬܐ ܕܡ̈ܠܟܐ . ܚܐܪ ܗ̣ܘܐ ܕܝܢ ܦܪ̈ܘܣܐ ܕܢܣܒ ܠܗܘܕܩ ܦܘ̈ܩܕܗ ܕܡܠܟܘܬܐ ܡܢ ܒܢ̈ܝܗ̇ ܕܡܕܝܢܬܐ: ܘܗܘܕܝܢ ܢܬܒ ܥܠ ܡܠܟܘܬܐ ܕܡ̈ܠܟܐ . ܕܠܡܐ ܢܬܒܥ. ܒܬܒ̈ܝܗ ܕܡܠܟܘܬܐ . ܦܪ̈ܘܣܐ ܘܠܐ ܡ̈ܠܟܐ . ܘܟܕ ܘܗܘܐ ܠܗ ܕܝܢ ܒܬ̈ܪ ܙ̇ܘܗܡܐ ܘܐܡܪ̇ܝܢ . ܐܢ ܦܘ̈ܩܕܗ ܠܡ ܕܡܠܟܘܬܐ ܬܬܒܥ ܡܢܝ . ܗܒ ܫܘܕܝܐ ܥܠ ܫܬ̈ܠܬܢ ܘܗܒ ܦܘ̈ܩܕܗ . ܐܡܪ ܠܗܘܢ ܠܗܠܝܢܘܢ . ܡܢܐ ܗܝ ܫܐܠܬܟܘܢ . ܐܡܪ̇ܝܢ ܠܗ . ܕܢܡܠܟ ܫܢܝܐ ܥܠ ܟܠ ܕܬ̈ܠܝ . ܗܠܝܢܘܢ ܕܝܢ ܐܢܫ ܒܪ̈ܝܫܗ ܘܫܬܩ . ܗܢܘܢ ܕܝܢ ܙ̇ܒܢܝܢ ܗܘܘ ܥܠܘܗܝ . ܘܩܒ̣ܠ ܒܗ ܐܡܪ̇ܝܢ . ܥܠ ܒܘܪ̇ܟܗ̇ ܕܡܠܟܘܬܢ ܪ̈ܓܐ ܐܢܬ ܠܡܬܒ . ܫܒܘܩ ܕܬ̈ܠܬܐ ܒܕܝܠܗܝܢ . ܘܐܢܬ ܐܝܟ ܕܫܦܪ ܠܟ ܒܬܪ ܒܕܝܠܟ: ܘܐܢ ܡܕܝܢܬ ܫܦܪ ܠܟ ܕܬܗܘܐ . ܙ̇ܘܦܢܐ ܕܒܢܬ ܡܥܡܕܝܢܘܗ ܢܬܒܥܐ ܡܢ ܡܠܟܘܬܐ . ܘܗܘܐ ܚܝ ܠܟ ܚ̈ܒܪܐ . ܒܗܠܝܢ ܪ̈ܓܫܐ ܡܕܝܢܬܢ . ܠܗܠܝܢ ܫ̈ܠܡܐ ܐܢܫܘܬܢ . ܦܐܝܐ ܠܒܘܢ ܒܢܝ

ܡܠܟܘܬܐ. ܟܕ ܬܬܒܪܘܢ ܫܠܡܐ ܒܐܘܚܕܢܗܘܢ. ܗܪܪܝ ܠܗܘܢ ܬܓܐ ܘܫܘܠܛܢܐ. ܟܕ ܡܪܚܡܢܘܬܗܘܢ ܬܬܦܪܣ ܥܠ ܟܠ ܫܘܝܐܝܬ. ܘܟܕ ܟܕܢܐ ܗܟܢܐ ܒܡܠܝܢ ܩ̈ܢܝܬ ܩ̈ܠܐ ܒܬܚܝܢ ܗܘܘ. ܐܡܪ ܠܗܘܢ ܦܪܘܩܐ ܗܕܐ ܐܝܟ ܕܫܬܘܢ ܠܗܘܢ: ܘܟܕ ܫܬܘ ܘܟܦܠܘ. ܡܠܠ ܒܗܡܘܢ ܘܐܡܪ ܠܗܘܢ. ܡܢܘ ܠܡ ܫܘܚܠܦܐ ܗܢܐ ܒܢܫܐ. ܕܐܚܕ ܠܗ ܠܡܪܕܝܬܗܘܢ. ܠܐ ܝܕܥܝܢ ܓܒܪ ܫܘܪܝܐ ܘܒܢ̈ܝܬܐ ܕܐܫܬܦܪ ܒܗ. ܘܐܦ ܡܢܟܐ ܡܠܟܘܬ ܬܒܘܒ ܫܘܪ̈ܝܢܝܗܘܢ ܘܫܘܒܚ̈ܐ ܕܒܢ̈ܝܬܗܘܢ: ܠܡܫܝܚ: ܡܫܬܚܪܝܢ ܡܢ ܣ̈ܓܝܢ: ܚܕܐ ܡܢ ܬܠܬ ܡܢ̈ܘܬܐ ܕܒܡܘܪ̈ܝܗ ܕܡܪܕܝܬܗܘܢ. ܐܠܐ ܡܛܠ ܕܫܘܪܝܐ ܗ̣ܝ ܕܡܠܟܘܬܐ. ܐܬܚܙܝܬ ܠܝ ܕܦܐܝܐ ܠܝ ܠܡܐ. ܕܒܒܪ ܫܘܒܚܐ ܠܣ̈ܒܐ ܟܕ ܝܗܒ. ܘܢܦܩܝ ܪ̈ܘܚܐ ܥܠ ܡܩ̈ܒܠܢܐ. ܗܕܐ ܕܝܢ ܬܬܝܕܥ ܠܟܘܢ ܟ̈ܠ ܪܗܘܡܝܐ. ܕܚܕܐ ܗܝ ܫܒܝܬ ܫܘܒܚܐ ܠܡܪܕܝܬܗܘܢ: ܡܢ ܗܫܐ ܕܝܢ ܠܝܬ ܫܘܒܚܐ ܘܠܐ ܪ̈ܘܡܐ. ܐܦܠܐ ܚ̈ܝܐ ܠܟܘܢ ܕܡܡܪܝܢ ܘܕܐܫ ܦܘܕܢܐ ܕܫܘܠܛܢ.

ܦܪܘܩܐ ܕܝܢ ܠܝܠܐ: ܡܢ ܒܬܪ ܕܐܫܬܠܡ ܠܦܘܠܚܢܐ ܐܘܣܦܘ: ܬ̈ܒܪܐ ܘܐܘܠ̈ܝܢܐ ܕܥܠ ܐܘܟ̈ܠܡܝܢ: ܘܚܙܝܐ ܕܠܐ ܐܬܦܪܥ ܠܝܚܝܕܗ. ܘܠܐ ܐܬܦܪܫ ܡܢ ܫܪܪܗ.

ܘܕܢܚܬ ܠܗ ܒܢܝܐ ܐܚܪ̈ܢܐ ܠܐ ܡܫܟܚ ܗܘܐ. ܐܬܟܬܫ ܗܘܐ ܠܗ ܥܡ ܦܓܪܗ ܕܡܕܒܪܢܐ. ܡܢ ܒܢ̈ܝܐ ܘܡܢ ܐܘ̈ܠܨܢܐ ܘܡܢ ܡܣܟ̈ܢܘܬܐ. ܘܟܕ ܒܠܥܘܗܝ ܦܘܪܢܐ ܡܟܘܬܐ ܕܣܘܦܐ. ܠܐ ܕܝܢ ܢܦܩ ܠܗ ܐܠܗܐ ܪܓܠܬܗ ܠܡܠܟܝ ܐܦ. ܠܐ ܒܗܕܐ. ܘܟܕ ܐܪܝܡ ܐܣܩܠܦܪܐ ܩܕܫܐ ܕܢܟܣܘܗܝ. ܐܬܦܫܪܬ ܚܪܡܗ ܘܢܦܠܬ ܡܕܡܘܗܝ.. ܐܝܟ ܕܡܬܦܫܪܐ ܫܥܘܬܐ ܡܢ ܡܢ ܢܘܪܐ. ܘܠܐ ܐܬܘܒ ܡܕܡܐ. ܠܐ ܓܝܪ ܢܩܦ. ܙܒܢܐ ܟܠܗ ܠܡܬܘܬܐ ܕܢܟܠܝܗ ܟܠ ܚܫܐ. ܒܕܡܐ ܕܥܒܕ ܟܦܢܐ ܕܐܟܠܗ ܕܠܘܗ ܕܪܥܝܐ. ܒܪ ܕܝܢ ܐܬܚܝܡ ܒܗ ܒܣܘܟܠܐ ܗܘ ܗܢܐ ܚܪܡܐ ܠܦܠܐ: ܕܠܐ ܢܘܪܐ ܐܟܠܬܗ ܘܠܐ ܚܘܬܐ ܡܪܒܬ ܠܗ. ܘܒܐܬ̈ܒܒܝܢ ܫܢ̈ܝܢ ܕܣܟܠ: ܡܬܘܬܐ ܠܓܡܪ ܠܐ ܒܙܥ ܒܗ: ܘܩܢܦܗ ܚܣܡ ܟܠ ܕܒܝܢܗ ܡܢܝܐ ܗܘ. ܐܬܦܢܝ ܘܗܘܐ ܐܝܟ ܕ̈ܒܪܐ ܘܐܬܐܡܪ ܡܕܡܘܗܝ.. ܘܟܕ ܚܙܐ ܦܓܪܢܐ ܒܟܠܗܝܢ: ܘܐܕܪܟ ܘܐܡܬܪܪ ܕܒܪܢܝܗ ܕܡܕܒܪܐ ܡܢ ܥܡܠܐ ܗܘ. ܠܐ ܬܘܒ ܐܡܪܚ ܕܢܬܒܪܐ ܠܡܘܒܠܗ. ܐܠܐ ܒܒܥ ܚܡܬܗ ܘܐܗܡܠ ܡܢ ܬܟܒܬܗ. ܘܒܢܝܗܝ ܡܢ ܡܕܡܘܗܝ. ܘܢܗܡܟ ܒܢܝܬ ܐܘܪܚܐ. ܒܪ ܡܣܬܡ ܠܒܥܘܗ ܠܡܣܟ̈ܢܘܬܐ: ܘܠܒ̈ܢܘܗܝ ܠܥܘܪ̈ܐ ܘܡܕ̈ܒܪܘܗܝ ܠܒܢ̈ܝܐ.

ܟܕ ܕܡܛܐ ܠܡܕܝܢܬܐ ܡܢ ܒܒܠ. ܠܐ ܕܝܢ ܐܫܬܘܝ ܡܒܝܢܗ ܡܫܝܚܐ ܕܡܓܠܠܬܗ ܘܟܠ ܢܦܫܐ. ܕܒܗ ܟܠܠܝܐ ܘܟܪܗ ܒܝܬ ܐܘܪܝܐ. ܘܐܣܠܩ ܒܐܪܥܬܗ، ܘܐܘܦ ܒܡܪܘܬܗ. ܐܡܒܝܐ ܕܐܦ ܠܐ ܚܕܐ ܫܡܥܬܐ ܡܬܚܙܝܐ ܗܘܬ ܒܟܠܗ ܠܒܝܫܘܬܗ. ܘܢܦܫ ܘܡܠܝܚ، ܪܘܚܐ ܕܒܫܝܢܐ ܘܒܠܒܘܫܬܐ. ܘܐܦܘܗ ܡܢ ܒܝܬ ܫܒܘܫܝܗ ܒܬܪܒܐ ܐܚܪܢܐ. ܘܐܦܝܢܗ ܡܢܗܘܢ، ܕܠܦܘܠܐ: ܒܪ ܢܦܫܝ ܥܠ ܐܦܘܗܝ، ܘܗܘܐ ܫܠܝܢܐ. ܗܒܢܐ ܕܝܢ ܬܡܢܝܢܗ ܗܘܐ ܫܘܗܝ. ܕܐܦ ܗܘ ܦܘܠܐ ܒܪ ܫܢܝܗ، ܗܘܐ. ܐܬܬܚܕ ܘܐܬܬܪܗܒ ܡܢ ܡܒܘܗܝ. ܘܒܪ ܗܘܐ ܠܒܪ ܕܫܢܘܐ ܢܚܐ ܗܘܐ. ܠܐ ܠܒܪ ܡܕܪܫܐ ܗܘܬ ܠܗ ܕܗܘܘܢ. ܒܒܢܝܐ ܕܥܒܪ ܒܒܢܝܗ، ܒܝܬ ܐܘܪܝܐ ܘܠܐ ܐܡܒܝܢܗ. ܬܡܢܝܗ ܗܘܐ ܕܝܢ ܦܘܠܐ ܘܬܘܪ ܥܠ ܬܫܡܫܬܐ ܕܒܐܪܥܐ، ܡܕܝܢܐ ܐܘܪܫܠܡ. ܘܬܘܪܐ ܗܘܐ ܒܦܫܗ ܡܠܟܘܬܐ. ܒܠܠܐ ܚܕܐ ܗܘܐ ܕܐܡܒܝܐ ܢܦܩ ܗܘܐ ܡܢܗ ܕܦܘܠܐ. ܕܢܘܪܝܐ ܗܘܐ ܠܒܪ ܫܡܥܘܢ ܠܫܘܥܐ ܕܐܠܗܐ. ܡܬܒܝܢ ܗܘܐ ܡܢ ܚܘܠܬܗ ܐܦ ܡܢ ܒܝܬܐ ܒܠܗ ܕܡܕܝܢܬܐ. ܘܕܢܚܕ ܠܗ ܬܘܒ ܥܒܕܐ. ܢܦܩ ܗܘܐ ܡܢ ܗ، ܕܐܘܪܫܠܡ. ܘܒܪ ܒܗܠܝܢ ܦܘܠܐ ܪܒܐ ܗܘܐ ܥܒܝܕ. ܐܬܬܚܕ ܒܗ ܡܫܒܚܬܐ. ܕܒܟܠ ܫܘܒܚܐ

ܠܬܫܒܘܚܬܗ̇ ܟܠܗܘܢ ܕܡܕܝܢܬܐ. ܕܒܠܬ ܫܘܒܩܢܗܘܢ ܕܗܠܝܢ ܢܫܬܪܐ ܐܘܣܒܝܣ ܘܢܦܩ ܡܢ ܡܕܝܢܬܗ، ܒܫܠܡܐ. ܘܫܪܝ ܡܠܝܛܘܣ ܘܐܦܩ ܡܕܒܪܐܝܬ ܡܢ ܫܒܘܩܝܐ ܠܐܘܪܟܝܢܗ̇ ܕܗܝܡܢܘܬܐ. ܘܡܠܠ ܥܡܗܘܢ ܕܝܢܐ̇. ܘܐܝܟ ܕܠܐܢܫܐ ܕܟܠܗܝܢ ܐܬܟܢܫܘ ܟܕ ܠܗܘܢ ܫܘܒܩܢܐ ܒܗ ܐܡܪ. ܘܠܝܬܐ ܠܟ ܐܟܘܬܗ ܘܡܢ. ܕܟܠܗܝܢ ܐܬܪܘܬܐ ܒܡܫܝܚܘܬܗܘܢ ܗܕܐ: ܕܗܘܝܢ ܐܫܬܡܥܬ ܒܟܠ ܒܟܠ ܫܘܟܐܝܬ. ܐܝܟܢܐ ܕܦܪܫܐ ܡܫܝܚܘܬܗܘܢ ܕܠܗܘܢ ܕܟܠܗܝܢ ܟܠ ܦܠܚܐ ܘܟܠ ܒܢܝܐ. ܒܗ ܒܡܕܝܢܬܐ ܫܒܝܬ ܫܘܒܩܢܐ ܡܠܟܘܬ ܟܠ ܟܠܗ ܐܘܪܫܠܡ: ܒܠ ܐܝܠܝܢ ܕܟܠܗܘܢ ܐܘܬܒܪ ܒܗ ܘܡܢ. ܡܢ ܗܫܐ ܕܝܢ. ܐܢ ܡܢܝܢ ܐܢܫ ܕܢܬܚܫܚ ܒܟܢܫܐ ܡܕܡܝܐ ܕܡܬܒܟܝܢܘܬܐ. ܗܢܐ ܢܗܘ. ܕܗܘ ܒܡܫܝܚܘܬܐ ܡܪܐ ܒܠܗܘܢ، ܬܒܥܬܐ ܕܥܒܕܐ ܕܒܒܪ. ܘܫܪܝ ܡܠܝܛܘܣ ܐܦܩ ܠܟܠܗܘܢ ܫܒܘܩܝܐ ܕܡܕܝܢܬܐ. ܘܒܝܕ ܦܘܪܣܐ ܕܡܬܬܒܥ ܐܬܬܪ، ܐܘܣܒܝܣ ܘܢܦܩ ܡܢ ܡܕܝܢܬܗ، ܒܡ ܗܠܝܢ ܫܬܬܟܢ ܘܬܫܒܘܚܬܗ̇ ܕܡܕܝܢܬܐ. ܒܗ ܡܘܗܝ ܘܡܫܒܚܝܢ ܠܐܠܗܐ. ܦܘܠܚܐ ܕܝܢ ܐܘܣܒܝܣ. ܒܗ ܒܟܠܠܐ ܡܘܕܐ ܗܘܐ ܒܠ ܢܦܫܗ ܕܪܘܣܦܢܝܐ ܗܘ. ܘܠܐ ܥܠܝ ܗܘܐ ܡܢ ܡܠܦܢܘܬܗ. ܘܕܠܐ ܕܢܠܬܐ ܘܡܢܦܐ ܡܫܒܚ ܗܘܐ

ܠܐܠܗܐ ܙܗܝܐܝܬ. ܘܢܦܩ ܡܢ ܢܦܩ ܥܠ ܕܒܪ̈ܘܗܝ ܐܠܗ̈ܐ ܡܫܡܫ ܗܘܐ. ܒܕܡܐ ܠܢܡܘܣܬܐ ܐܣܝܪܝܬܐ.

ܗܘ ܕܝܢ ܦܘܠܚܢܐ ܐܘܣܟܡܝܣ ܒܢ̈ܝܢܐ. ܒܕܡܐ ܕܢܒܝܒ ܦܝܠܐ ܕܡܫܘܬܗ ܕܝܘܠܦܢܗ ܒܦܠܐ: ܘܫܕܝܬ ܘܪܘܬ ܪܘܫܡ ܒܦܘܪܢܐ ܕܒܢ̈ܝ ܐܠܗܐ ܠܒܢ̈ܝܗ. ܘܐܬܒܢܝܐܬ ܗܝܟܠܘܬܗ ܒܦܬܫܡܝܢ ܕܒܪ̈ܬܐ: ܘܒܦܘܢܝܐ ܕܦ̈ܘܢܝܗܝܢ. ܘܒܢܘܫܢܐ ܕܦ̈ܠܓܝܗܝܢ. ܘܒܣܝܒܘܬܐ ܦܠܒܬܐ ܥܠ ܒܪܬܐ ܕܢܝܫܦ ܗܘ̣ܐ ܒܡܢܫܗ ܡܢ ܒܠܒܐ̣. ܒܫܢܬ ܫܬܡܐܐ ܘܫܒܥܝܢ ܘܬܠܬ ܒܡܢܝܢܐ ܕܝ̈ܘܢܝܐ ܕܐܝܬܝܗ̇ ܫܢܬ ܬܠܬ ܡܐܐ ܘܫܬܝܢ ܘܫܒܥ. ܒܡܠܟܘܬܗ ܕܡܪܢ ܝܫܘܥ ܕܒܝܬ ܢ̈ܘܗܪ ܐܒܫܐ. ܗ̇ܘ ܕܠܗ ܘܠܐܒܘܗܝ ܘܠܪܘܚ ܩܘܕܫܗ. ܫܘܒܚܐ ܘܐܝܩܪܐ ܘܣܓܕܬܐ ܗܫܐ ܘܒܟܠܙܒܢ ܘܠܥܠܡ ܥܠܡܝܢ ܐܡܝܢ.

ABBREVIATIONS

a = afᶜel
a = imperfect in a
ad = adjective
av = adverb
c = cum
cm = common gender
co = conjuction
eš = eštafᶜal
et = ethpeᶜel
etp = ethpaᶜal
eta = ettafᶜal
f = feminine
in = interjection
N = NÖLDEKE's *Syrische Grammatik*[2]
n = noun
p = plural
pa = paᶜel
pe = peᶜal
pas = passive
pr = preposition
pt = participle
tr = transitive
s. v. = sub voce
u = imperfect in u
v = verb

GLOSSARY.

ܐ

ܐܒܐ (abbā) p. ܐܒܗܬܐ (abbahāthā) father — *Vater*

ܐܒܕ (ebhadh) perish — *zu Grunde gehen*; ܐܒܕܢܐ (abhdānā) destruction — *Untergang*

ܐܒܠܐ (ebhlā) mourning — *Trauer*

ܐܓܘܢܐ (agōnā) ܐܝܓܘܢܐ (igōnā) ἀγών contest — *Streit, Kampf*

ܐܓܘܢܣܛܐ (agonesṭa) ἀγωνιστής champion — *Verteidiger* ܐܓܘܢܝܣܛܘܬܐ (agonisṭūthā) championship — *Verteidigung*

ܐܓܪ (egar) eta. gain — *gewinnen*; ܐܓܪܐ (agrā) payment — *Bezahlung*; ܐܬܓܘܪܬܐ, ܬܓܘܪܬܐ (tēgurtā) commerce, traffic — *Handel*; ܬܓܪܐ (taggārā) trafficer (in a spiritual sense) — *Handelsmann (im geistlichen Sinn)*

ܐܕܢܐ (edhnā) ear — *Ohr*

6

ܐܘܕܩܛܘܣ Adocetus

ܐܘܛܘܩܪܛܘܪ αὐτοκράτωρ

ܐܘܝܘܬܐ (awyūthā) accord — *Einklang*

ܐܘܣܒܝܣ Eusebius

ܐܘܣܝܐ (ūsiyā) p. ܐܘܣܝ̈ܣ (ūsiyūs) οὐσία property — *Eigentum*

ܐܙܠ (ezal) go — *gehen*; ܡܐܙܠܬܐ (mezalthā) journey, life-journey — *Lebenslauf*

ܐܚܐ (aḥā) brother — *Bruder*

ܐܚܕ (eḥadh) seize, take up — *ergreifen;* ܐ' ܥܩܒܐ follow — *nachfolgen;* ܐ' ܬܪܥܐ shut the gate — *d. Thor Schliessen*; ܐܚܝܕ (aḥīdh) tr. c. acc. et ܠ, take hold of, hold — *ergreifen, halten*; ܐܚܝܕܐ (ahīdhā) possessor — *Besitzer, Inhaber*; ܐܘܚܕܢܐ (uḥdānā) Kingdom — *Reich*

ܐܚܪܝܐ (ḥerāyā) f. ܐܚܪܝܬܐ (ḥeraitā) ad. last — *letzter*

ܐܟ (āḥ) as — *wie*; with numerals "about" — *mit Zahlen "etwa"*; ܕܐܟܘܬܟ like thee — *dir ähnlich*; ܐܟ ܕ as, so that (N. §. 364 B), as if, for the purpose of — *wie, so dass, als wie, damit*

ܐܝܟܐ where — *wo*; ܠܐܝܟܐ whither — *wohin*

ܐܝܟܢܐ (aikanā) how — *wie*; ܐܝܟܢܐ ܕ so that — *damit*

ܐܝܢܐ (ainā) f. ܐܝܕܐ p. cm. ܐܝܠܝܢ (ailēn) that one, those — *welcher*, *jener*; ܗܘ ܐܝܢܐ ܕ he that — *derjenige welcher*

ܐܝܬ v. is — *ist*; ܕܐܝܬܘܗܝ (dīthē) id est; ܐܝܬ ܠܗ ܕ had in his power to — *besass die Macht dass*

ܐܟܣܘܪܝܐ ἐξορία exile — *Verbannung*

ܐܟܣܪܟܐ, ܐܟܣܪܟܘܣ ἔξαρχης

ܐܟܦ (ekhaph) urge — *dringen auf, in*

ܐܟܪܐ (akkārā) husbandman — *Landmann*

ܐܠܐ but — *aber*; ܐܠܐ ܐܢ (N. § 374 D) except — *wenn nicht, ausgenommen*

ܐܠܗܐ (allāhā) God — *Gott*; p. the gods — *die Götter*; ܐܠܗܝܐ (allāhāyā) ad. godly — *göttlich*

ܐܠܦ (ālāph) 1000

ܐܠܨ (elaṣ) be necessary — *notwendig sein*; ܐܘܠܨܢܐ (ulṣānā) hardship, tribulation — *Qual, Not*

ܐܡܐܪܐ p. ܐܡܪ̈ܣ ἀμάρα sewer — *Rinne*

ܐܡܝܢܐ (ammīnā) ad. faithful, unremitting — *treu, beständig*

ܐܡܪ (emar) say — *sagen*

ܐܡܪܐ (emrā) sheep — *Lamm*

ܐܡܬܝ (ēmath) when, whenever — *wann, so oft*; ܐܡܬܝ ܕ when — *wann*

ܐܢ if — *wenn*

ܐܢܚ etp. groan — *seufzen*

ܐ̄ܢܫܐ (nāšā) man, men, anyone, someone — *Mensch, Menschen, irgend Einer, jemand*; ܐ̄ܢܫ ܐ̄ܢܫ each one — *jeder*; ܒܪ ܐܢܫܐ man — *Mensch*; ܐ̄ܢܫܘܬܐ (nāšūthā) inhabitants — *Einwohner*

ܐ̄ܢܬ (at) thou — *du*

ܐ̄ܢܬܬܐ (attā) p. ܢܫ̈ܐ (nešē) woman, wife — *Frau, Weib*

ܐܣܐ pa. heal — *heilen*

ܐܣܟܝܡܐ, ܐܣܟܡܐ (eskīmā) σχῆμα kind, garb — *Weise, Gewand*

ܐܣܦܩܠܛܪܐ (aspeklaṭra) σπεκουλάτωρ lictor

ܐܣܝܪܐ s. v. ܒܝܬ

ܐܦ (āph) av. also — *auch*; ܐܦܠܐ not even, neither — *nicht ein mal*; ܐܦܢ (aphen = ܐܦ ܐܢ, N. § 374 E) even if — *wenn auch*

ܐܦ̈ܐ (appē) face — *Gesicht*; ܢܣܒ ܐ' s. v. ܢܣܒ; ܠܐܦ̈ܝ (lappai) to — *zu*; ܥܠ ܐܦ̈ܝ because of, for — *wegen, für*

ܐܦܘܠܘ Apollo

ܐܦܝܢܛܘܣ Epänetus

ܐܦܝܣܩܘܦܐ (apiskopā) ἐπίσκοπος bishop — *Bischof*

ܐܦܪܣܢܐ (āpharsānā) machinations — *Anstiftungen*

ܐܪܒܥܝܢ 40; ܐܪܒܥܡܐܐ 400

ܐ̄ܪܙܐ s. v. ܪܐܙܐ

ܐܪܡܠܬܐ (armeltā) widow — *Wittwe*

ܐܪܥ s. v. ܦܪܣܐ

ܐܪܥܐ land — *Land*

ܐܫܕ (eshadh) shed (blood) — (*Blut*) *vergiessen*; et. be poured out — *ausgegossen sein*

ܐܫܟܪܐ (eškārā) field — *Acker*

ܐܬܐ (ethā) come, follow — *kommen*, *folgen*; a. bring — *bringen*; ܡܐܬܝܬܐ (mēthīthā) n. coming — *Kommen, Ankunft*

ܐܬܠܝܛܐ ἀθλητής wrestler (in spiritual sense) — *Kämpfer* (*im geistigen Sinn*); ܐܬܠܝܛܘܬܐ fortitude — *Tapferkeit*

ܐܬܪܐ (athrā) (N. § 70 Bi) p. ܐܬܪ̈ܘܬܐ (athrawāthā) place, country, occasion — *Ort*, *Land*, *Gelegenheit*

ܒ

ܒ pr. in, because of, according to, through, on, despite — *in, wegen, nach, durch, auf, nichts desdoweniger;* ܒܬܠܬܝܢ 30 times — 30 *Mal;* ܒܗ ܒܠܠܝܐ in that same night — *in der selbigen Nacht;* ܒܕ since — *da*

ܒܐܫ, ܒܝܫܐ (bīšā) n. wrong, hardship, evil person — *Bedrückung, Beschwerden, böser Mensch;* ad. wicked — *gottlos*

ܒܗܠ (b^{e}hel) become quiet — *ruhig werden*

ܒܗܬ (b^{e}heth) a. put to shame — *beschämen*

ܒܘܠܘܣܝܢܘܣ Volusianus

ܒܙ (baz) v. plunder — *plündern*

ܒܙܚܐ (bezḥā) ignominy — *Schande*

ܒܚܪ (b^{e}ḥar) et. be proven — *bewiesen sein*

ܒܛܠ (b^{e}ṭel) perish — *aufhören, untergehen;* ܒܛܝܠܘܬܐ (b^{e}ṭīlūthā) opinion, state of mind, dilligence — *Meinung, Sinn, Fleiss*

ܒܝܐ (bayyā) pa. console — *trösten;* etp. be consoled — *getröstet sein;* ܒܘܝܐܐ (buyā'ā) consolation — *Trost*

ܒܝܬܐ (baita) house — *Haus*; ܒ' ܐܠܗܐ the faithful — *die Gläubigen*; ܒ' ܐܣܝܪ̈ܐ prison — *Gefängniss*; ܒ' ܢܛܘܪܬܐ prison cell — *Zelle*; ܒ' ܚܙܘܢ̈ܐ (ḥezwānē) theatre — *Theater*; ܒ' ܟܢܘܫܬܐ gathering place — *Versammelungsort*; ܒ' ܦܬܟܪ̈ܐ, ܒ' ܓܠܝ̈ܐ heathen tempel — *heidnische Tempel*; ܒ' ܥܒܪܐ Synagogue — *Synagoge*; co. (N. § 251) among, in — *zwischen, in*; ܒܝܬ . . . . ܠ between . . . . and — *zwischen . . . und*; ܒܝܬ among — *zwischen*

ܒܢ (bān) etp. understand — *verstehen, erkennen*

ܒܝܢ (bain) between — *zwischen*; ܒܝܢܝ ܘܠܟ (bainai welākh N. § 251) between me and you — *zwischen mir und dir*

ܒܟܐ weep — *weinen*; pa. lament — *beweinen, klagen*

ܒܘܟܪ̈ܐ (bukhrā) first-born — *Erstgeborener*

ܒܠܗܝ (balhi) astonish, astound — *in Erstaunung setzen*; ܒܘܠܗܝܐ (bulhāyā) Stupefaction — *Betäubung*

ܒܠܥ inhale — *einatmen*

ܒܠܥܕ ܡܢ (bel'ūd men) without — *ohne*

ܒܢܐ build — *bauen*; ct. be built, rebuilt — *gebaut, wieder-*

gebaut sein; ܒܢܝܢܐ (benyānā) act of building — *das Bauen*

ܒܣܒܣ (basbes) etp. tear in pieces — *zerreisen*

ܒܣܡ etp. be entertained — *unterhalten sein;* ܒܣܝܡܐ (bassīmā) ad. benevolent — *wohlwollend*

ܒܥܐ search — *suchen, trachten;* ܒܥܬܐ (be^{c}āthā) search, debate — *das Suchen, Debatte*

ܒܥܠܕܒܒܐ (b$^{e c}$eld^{e}bhābhā) enemy — *Feind*

ܒܨܐ scrutinise — *erforschen, prüfen;* et. be examined — *geprüft werden*

ܒܨܪ diminish, lessen — *verringern;* etp. be diminished — *verringert werden*

ܒܘܩܝܐ (būḳḳāyā) probation — *Probe*

ܒܪܐ son — *Sohn;* ܒܢ̈ܝ inhabitants of — *Einwohner von;* ܒܪܢܫܐ man — *Mensch;* ܒܪ ܒܝܬܐ servant — *Diener;* ܒ' ܪܢܝܐ of the same mind — *dergleichen Meinung;* ܒ' ܐܪ̈ܙܐ one initiated into the mysteries — *der in die Geheimnisse Eingeführt;* ܒܪܬ ܩܠܐ (bath ḳālā) p. ܒܢ̈ܬ ܩܠܐ (benāth ḳālā) word — *Wort*

ܒܪ, ܠܒܪ outside — *ausserhalb;* ܠܒܪ ܡܢ outside — *ausser;* ܒܪܝܐ (barrāyā) ad. outer — *äusserer*

ܒܪܝܬܐ (berithā) creation, creature — *Schöpfung*, *Creatur*;

ܒܪܘܝܐ (bārōyā) creator — *Schöpfer*

ܒܪܟ ܡܒܪܟܐ (mebharrekhā) part. pas. ad. blessed — *gesegneter*; ܒܪܝܟܐ (berīkhā) ad. id.; etp. be blessed — *gesegnet sein*

ܒܪܡ (beram) but — *aber*

ܒܪܝܪܐ (barrīrā) ingenuous — *schlicht, einfältig*

ܒܪܨ (beraṣ) c. ܒ (pierce) enter — *eintreten*

ܒܬܪ (bāthār) after — *nach*; ܡܢ ܒܬܪ ܕ after that — *nachdem*; ܕܡܢ ܒܬܪܟܡ ad. subsequent — *folgend*

ܓ

ܓܒܐ pa. choose — *wählen*; pt. pas. ܓܒܝܐ ܗܘ ܠܝ I would choose — *ich möchte wählen*

ܓܒܪܐ (gabhrā) man — *Mann*; ܓܒܪܘܬܐ (gabbārūthā) fortitude — *Tapferkeit*

ܓܕܫ (gedhaš) *a* happen — *geschehen*

ܓܘܐ (gawwā) the inside — *das Innerer*; ܠܓܘ, (legau) ܠܓܘ ܡܢ pr. within — *innerhalb*; ܓܘܝܐ (gawwāyā) ad. inward — *innerer*

ܓܙܐ (gazā) treasure — *Schatz*

7

ܓܙܒܪܐ (gezabhrā) treasurer — *Schatzmeister*

ܓܙܡܐ (gezāmā) threat — *Drohung*

ܓܙܪ ܕܝܢܐ ܓܙܪ judgement — *Gericht*

ܓܙܪܐ (gezārā) flock — *Herde*

ܓܝܪ (gēr) co. γάρ for, but, indeed — *denn, aber, wahrlich*

ܓܠܐ c. ܓܠ reveal — *enthüllen;* pa. ibid. — ܓܠܝܐ (galyā) pe. pt. pas. open — *offen;* ܐܦܐ ܓܠܝܬܐ (appē galyāthā) confidence — *Vertrauen;* ܥܝܢ ܒܓܠܐ (ʿēn bagelē) face to face, openly — *vor Angesicht zur Angesicht, offen;* ܓܠܝܐܝܬ (galyā'īth) av. openly — *öffentlich*

ܓܠܙ (gelaz) despoil — *berauben;* et. be despoiled — *beraubt werden*

ܓܠܝܘܣ Gallius, Gaul — *Gallien*

ܓܠܝܦܐ (gelīphā) idol — *Götze*

ܓܡܪ *u* work, produce, carry-out — *arbeiten, einbringen, durchführen;* et. be finished — *vollendet werden;* ܓܡܝܪܐ (gemīrā) ad. exquisite — *vorzüglich;* ܓܡܪܐ (gemārā) perfection — *Vollendung;* ܠܓܡܪ (lagemar) av. entirely — *durchaus;* ܠܓܡܪ ܠܐ in no way — *auf keine Weise*

ܓܦ a. ܐܓܦ ܐܝܕܐ ܥܠ cover with the hand — *mit der Hand bedecken*

ܓܢܒ (g^e^nabh) *u* steal — *stehlen*

ܓܒܐ (gabbā) side (of body) — *Seite* (*des Körpers*); party — *Partei*

ܓܥܫ et. be moved (in mind or heart); be pained — *gerührt, beleidigt, gekränkt werden*

ܓܥܐ groan — *seufzen, stöhnen*

ܓܥܠ (g^e^ʿal) a. entrust — *anvertrauen*; et. pass.

ܓܥܪ c. ܒ rebuke — *tadeln*

ܓܪܐ pa. incite — *anreizen*

ܓܘܫܡܐ (gušmā) body — *Leib*

ܕ

ܕ for, since, because — *da, weil*; introduces direct discourse — *leitet die directe Rede ein* (N § 367); ܕܠܐ without — *ohne*

ܕܐܒܐ (debhā) wolf — *Wolf*

ܕܒܚ ܕܒܚܐ (debhḥā) Sacrifice — *Opfer*; ܡܕܒܚܐ (madhb^e^ḥā) altar — *Altar*

ܕܒܪ ܕܘܒܪܐ (dubbārā) doings, manners — *Taten, Sitten*; ܡܕܒܪܢܐ (m^e^dhabb^e^rānā) leader — *Leiter*; ܡܕܒܪܢܘܬܐ (m^e^dhabb^e^rānūthā) leadership — *Leitung*

ܕܓܠ pa. c. ܒ deny — *verleugnen*

ܕܗܒܐ (dahbhā) gold — *Gold*

ܕܠ (dāl) a. excite — *anregen*

ܕܢ (dān) give judgement — *das Urteil sprechen*; eta. be judged — *verurteilt werden*

ܕܨ (dāṣ) exult — *frohlocken*

ܕܫ (dāš) tread, enter, tread under foot — *treten, eintreten, zertreten*

ܕܚܠ (deḥel) *a* fear — *fürchten*; ܕܚܠܐ (deḥlā) fear, worship, religion — *Furcht, Gottesdienst, Religion*

ܕܚܩ (deḥak) *u* push — *schieben*

ܕܝܠ (ܠ + ܕܝ) possessive particle — *selbständige possessivpronomen*; e. g. ܕܝܠܝ mine — *mein* (N §§ 69, 225 A)

ܕܝܢ (dēn) co. but, however — *aber, denn*

ܡܕܝܢܬܐ (medhittā) city — *Stadt*

ܕܝܪܐ (dairā) p. ܕܝܪܬܐ (dairāthā) convent — *Kloster*; ܕܝܪܝܐ (dairāyā) n. monk — *Mönch*

ܕܟܪ et. c. ܠ remind — *erinnern*; c. ܕ remember — *sich erinnern*; ܕܘܟܪܢܐ (dukhrānā) remembrance — *Gedächtniss*

ܕܠ ܕܠܝܠܐ (dallīlā) few — *wenig*

ܕܡ (dam) [ܡܐ + ܕ] lest, per chance (used after verbs of fearing) — *damit nicht, aus Furcht dass* N. § 373;

ܕܠܡܐ (dalmā) lest — *damit nicht, dass nicht*

ܕܡܐ (d^{e}mā) blood — *Blut*

ܕܡܐ resemble — *gleichen*; etp. c. ܒ imitate — *nachahmen*;

ܕܡܘܬܐ (d^{e}mūthā) image — *Bild, Vorbild*;

ܒܗ ܒܕܡܘܬܐ in the same manner — *gleichfalls*; ܒܕܡܘܬ co. like, as — *wie*

ܕܡܥܐ (demʿā) tear — *Thräne*

ܕܡܪ etp. be admired, be astonished, (c. ܒ) admire — *bewundert werden, erstaunt sein*, (c. ܒ) *bewunderen*

ܕܪܐ (d^{e}rā) cast — *werfen*

ܕܪܪܐ (darrā) n. fight — *Kampf*

ܕܪܓܐ (dargā) station, position — *Stufe, Rang*

ܕܪܟ *a* befall, come to the aid of, understand — *sich ereignen, Hilfe leisten, begreifen*

ܕܪܫ (d^{e}raš) *a* study — *studieren*; pa. pas. pt. expert, skilled — *gewandt*

ܕܘܫܢܐ (dūšnā) gift — *Gabe*

ܗ

ܗܐ inter. behold! — *Siehe!*

ܗܒܒ pa. flourish — *gedeihen*

ܗܕܡܐ (haddāmā) member, part (of body), part of speech, word — *Glied (des Körpers), Redetheil, Wort*

ܗܕܪ ܗܕܝܪܐ (hedhīrā) ad. beautiful — *schön*

ܗܘ pro. he — *er*; used enclitically for emphasis — *enclitisch gebraucht um einen Wort hervorzuheben* (N § 221); ܕܗܘܝܘ that it was he — *dass er es war*

ܗܘܐ be, exist — *sein*; used enclitically — *enclitisch gebraucht* (N. § 263); ܡܢ ܟܝ ܗܘܐ (mān kai hewā) what had become — *was geschehen war*

ܗܘܦܛܝܘܣ ὑπατεία consular largess — *Geschenke vor dem Consul ausgestreut*

ܗܝܕܝܢ (haidēn) then — *darauf*

ܗܝܟܠܐ (haiklā) temple — *Tempel*

ܗܝܡܢ (haimen) etp. be believed — *geglaubt werden*; ܡܗܝܡܢܐ (mehaimnā) pt. n. trusted person, minister, believer, Christian — *Anvertrauter, Minister, Gläubiger, Christ*; ܗܝܡܢܘܬܐ (haimānūthā) faith — *Glaube*

ܗܟܝܠ (hākhēl) therefore — *also*

ܗܟܢܐ (hākhanā) thus — *so*

ܗܠ a. c. ܒ scoff at — *verspotten*

ܗܦܐ a. avert (eyes) — (*die Augen*) *abwenden*; c. ܡܢ desist, abandon — *absehen von, aufgeben*

ܗܢܐ f. ܗܕܐ p. ܗܠܝܢ pro. demonstr.; ܗܢܘ (hānau) (= ܗܘ + ܗܢܐ) that — *jene*

ܗܦܟ (hephakh) c. ܠ return — *zurückkehren*; c. ܡܢ turn from — *sich wenden von*; a. turn away, avert (face), answer — *umkehren, (das Gesicht) abwenden, antworten*; et. turn — *umschlagen*

ܗܪܓ (herag) et. meditate — *nachdenken*

ܗܫܐ (hāšā) s. v. ܫܥܐ

ܘ

ܘܝ (wai) woe! — *wehe*!

ܘܠܐ (wālē) pt. it is proper — *es ziemt*, c ܠ person; ܘܠܝܬܐ (wālīthā) propriety — *Anstand, Schicklichkeit*

ܘܥܕ ܥܕܬܐ (ʿedhtā) p. ܥܕܬ̈ܐ (ʿedhāthā) church — *Kirche*

ܙ

ܙܒܢܐ (zabhnā) time — *Zeit*; ܟܠܙܒܢ always — *immer*; ܚܕܐ ܙܒܢ for once — *für Einmal*

ܙܒܢ (zebhan) buy — *kaufen*

ܙܕܩ pa. justify — *rechtfertigen*; ܙܕܝܩܘܬܐ (zaddīḳūthā) righteousness — *Gerechtigkeit*

ܙܗܝܐ ܙܗܝܐܝܬ (zahyā'īth) nobly, worthily — *herrlich, prächtig*

ܙܗܪ (z^e har) et. c. ܒ have a care for — *sich um ... Kümmern*;

ܙܗܝܪܐ (z^e hīrā) ad. brilliant — *glänzend*

ܙܘܕܐ (z^e wādhā) sustenance, victuals — *Nahrung, Kost*

ܙܘܚܐ (zauḥā) pomp — *Gepränge*

ܙܘܣ Ζεύς

ܙܥ (zā') et. be agitated, occur (to one's mind) — *aufgeregt sein, sich erinnern*; a. move (trans.) — *bewegen*; eta. tremble — *zittern*; ܙܘܥܬܐ (zū'thā) trembling — *das Zittern*

ܙܝܘܐ (zīwā) splendour — *Glanz, Pracht*

ܙܝܙܢܐ (zīzānā) ζιζάνιον tares — *Unkraut*

ܙܝܢܐ (zainā) arms — *Waffen*; pa. denom. arm — *waffnen*

ܙܟܐ be victorious — *besiegen*; ܙܟܘܬܐ (z^e khūthā) victory — *Sieg*

ܙܥܪ ܙܥܘܪܐ (z^e 'ōrā) few, small, short (time) — *wenige, klein, kurz (e Zeit)*; ܠܐ ܙܥܘܪ sufficiently — *genügend*

ܙܩܦ et. be crucified — *gekreuzigt werden*; ܙܩܘܦܐ (zāḳōphā) crucifier — *Kreuziger*

ܙܩܬ (z^e ḳath) stimulate — *anreizen*

ܙܪܥܐ (zar'ā) seed — *Same*

ܚ

ܚܐܦܐ (ḥephā) force — *Gewalt*

ܚܐܪܐ ܚܐܪܘܬܐ (hērūthā) liberty — *Freiheit*

ܚܒ. ܚܘܒܐ (ḥūbbā) love — *Liebe*; ܚܒܝܒܐ (ḥabbībhā) beloved — *geliebt*; ܚܒܝܒܐܝܬ (ḥabbībhāʾīth) lovingly — *freundlich*

ܚܒܠܐ (ḥebhālā) destruction — *Verderben*; ܚܒܠܗ ܠ (ḥebhālēh l...) woe to ...! — *wehe ...!*

ܚܒܪܐ (ḥabhrā) companion — *Genosse*

ܚܒܫ (ḥebhaš) *u* clap into prison — *ins Gefängniss werfen*; ܚܒܘܫܝܐ (ḥebhušyā) durance — *Gefangenschaft*

ܚܓܒ ܚܘܓܒܐ (ḥugbhā) oracle — *Weissagung*

ܚܕܐ ad. one — *ein*; av. in the first place — *erstens* (N § 243); ܚܕܐ ܡܢ ܬܠܬ ܡܢܘ̈ܬܐ 1/3; ܚܕ̈ܕܐ each other — *einander*; ܠܚܘܕ av. alone — *allein, nur*; ܒܠܚܘܕ (balehūdh) only — *nur*

ܚܕܝ (ḥedhī) rejoice — *sich freuen*

ܚܕܪܐ (ḥedhārā) neighbourhood — *Umgebung*

ܚܕܬ pa. renew, rejuvenate, invent — *erneuern, erfinden*

ܚܒ. (ḥābh) et. be owing — *ziemen*; ܚܝܒܐ (ḥayyābhā) guilty — *schuldig*

ܚܘܝ (ḥawwī) pa. show, exhibit, tell — *zeigen, erzählen;* ܬܚܘܝܬܐ (taḥwīthā) proof, example — *Beweis, Beispiel*

ܚܪ (ḥār) look, see, be on the watch, look upon (c. ܒ) — *blicken, sehen, lauern, ansehen* (c. ܒ); ܚܝܪܐ (ḥᵉyārā) sight — *Blick*

ܚܙܝ see — *sehen;* ܚ' ܒ look upon with satisfaction — *mit Genugthum sehen;* pt. pas. ܚܙܐ ܠ (ḥᵉzē l. . .) seen by — *gesehen von . . .;* et. be seen, appear, seem proper (c. ܠ) — *gesehen werden, erscheinen, recht scheinen* (c. ܠ); ܚܙܘܐ (ḥezwā) sight, appearance, vision — *Blick, Erscheinung, Vision;* ܚܙܬܐ (ḥᵉzāthā) sight — *Blick;* ܚܙܘܢܐ s. v. ܒܝܬ

ܚܙܡ pe. and pa. gird — *gürten*

ܚܛܐ v. sin — *sündigen;* ܚܛܗܐ (ḥᵉṭāhā), ܚܛܝܬܐ (ḥᵉṭīthā) sin — *Sünde*

ܚܘܛܪܐ (huṭrā) stave — *Stab*

ܚܝ̈ܐ (ḥayyē) life — *Leben;* ܚܝܘܬܐ (ḥayūthā) wild beast — *wildes Tier*

ܚܝܠܐ, ܚܝܠ (ḥēl, ḥailā) power, army (p. ܚܝ̈ܠܘܬܐ) — *Kraft, Heeresmacht;* ܚܝܠܬܢܐ (ḥailthānā) ad. lusty,

hardy — *kräftig, stark*; ܚܝܠܬܢܐܝܬ (ḥailthānā'ith) av. lustily — *kräftig*; v. denom. ܚܝܠ (ḥayyel) strengthen — *stärken*

ܚܟܡ (ḥekhem) understand — *verstehen*; ܚܟܡܬܐ (ḥekhmethā) wisdom — *Weisheit*; ܚܟܡܬܟ Thy Wisdom (honorific. appellation as "Thy Holiness") — *Deine Weisheit (ehrende Anrede wie "Deine Heiligkeit")*; ܒܚܟܝܡܐ av. cunningly — *geschickt*; ܚܟܝܡܐ (ḥakkīmā) ad. wise — *weise, klug*

ܚܠ ܚܘܠܢܐ (ḥūlānā) chasm in a rock — *Kluft*

ܚܠܛ mingle — *mischen*

ܚܠܡ ad. ܚܠܝܡܐ (ḥelīmā) perfect — *vollkommen*; v. a. cure — *heilen*

ܚܠܦ co. with or without suffix: for, in place of — *mit oder ohne suffix: für, anstatt*; ܒܚܠܦܐ ܕ (beḥelpā d....) in exchange for — *als ersatz für, dafür*; v. pa. change — *ändern*; ša. exchange — *vertauschen*; ܡܫܚܠܦܐ (mešaḥlephā) ad. various — *verschieden*

ܚܠܨ ܚܠܝܨܘܬܐ (ḥelīṣūthā) vigour — *Kraft*; ܚܠܝܨܐܝܬ av. vigourously — *kräftig*

ܚܡ ܚܘܡܐ (ḥūmā) heat — *Hitze*

ܚܡܒܐ go to ruin — *zu Grunde gehen*

ܚܡܣܢ (ḥamsen) persevere — *beharren*

ܚܡܫܐ 5; ܚܡܫܡܐܐ 500

ܚܡܬ etp. grow angry — *erzürnen*

ܚܢܦ ܚܢܦܐ (ḥanphā) pagan — *Heide*; ܚܢܦܘܬܐ (ḥanphūthā) heathenism — *Heidentum*

ܚܣܐ ܚܣܝ, ܚܣܝܐ (ḥesī, ḥasyā) n. holy man — *Heiliger*; ܚܣܝܘܬܐ (ḥasyūthā) holiness — *Heiligkeit*; ܚܣܝܘܬܟ "Thy Holiness" (honorific apellation) — "*Deine Heiligkeit*" (*ehrende Anrede*); ܡܚܣܝܐ (meḥasseyā; pa. pt. pas.) ad. innocent — *unschuldig*

ܚܣܟ et. be restrained — *zurückgehalten werden*

ܚܣܢ ܚܣܢ ܟܠ (ḥesen kul) ad. all-powerful — *allgewaltig*; ܠܡܚܣܢ (lemaḥsen) av. hardly — *kaum*

ܚܣܪ become less — *weniger werden*; pa. lack — *bedürfen*

ܚܦܛ pa exhort — *ermahnen*; ܡܚܦܛܢܘܬܐ (meḥaphṭānūthā) exhortation -- *Ermahnung*

ܚܪܐ et. desist — *abstehen von*

ܚܪܒ (ḥerebh) *a.* be deserted, go to ruin — *verlassen sein, zu Grunde gehen*; ܚܪܒ (ḥerabh) *u.* destroy — *vernichten*; et. be destroyed — *vernichtet werden*; a. destroy — *vernichten*; ܚܪܒܐ (ḥarbā) sword — *Schwert*

ܚܪܡܐ (ḥarmā) ad. accursed — *verflucht*

ܚܫ *a.* be pained — *leiden*; ܚܫܐ (ḥaššā) pain, ache — *Schmerz*; ܚܫܝܫܐ (ḥaššīšā) ad. troubled, cast down — *verdrossen, niedergeschlagen*; ܚܫܝܫܐܝܬ (ḥaššīšā'īth) av. grievously — *schmerzlich*

ܚܫܒ et. be counted — *gezählt werden*; ܚܘܫܒܐ (ḥūšābhā) thought — *Gedanke*; ܚܘܫܒܢܐ (ḥušbānā) account — *Rechnung*; ܡܚܫܒܬܐ (maḥšabhtā) thought — *Gedanke*

ܚܫܚ (ḥᵉšaḥ) be suitable, necessary — *passend, notwendig sein*; etp. c. ܒ make use of, act — *sich bedienen, tun*

ܚܬܡ (ḥᵉtham) *u.* make the sign of the cross over (c. acc. pers.)— *bekreuzigen* (c. acc. pers.)

ܚܬܪ ܚܬܝܪܘܬܐ (ḥᵉthīrūthā) haughtiness — *Stolz*; ܡܚܬܬܪܐ (meḥattᵉrā; pa. pt.) ad. puffed up — *aufgeblazen*

ܛ

ܛܒܐ (ṭebbā) report — *Nachricht*

ܛܒܒ v. coin — *münzen*

ܛܒ ܛܒܐ (ṭābhā) ad. good — *gut*; ܛܒ (ṭābh) av. exceedingly — *sehr*; ܛܘܒܐ (ṭūbhā) ܛ' ܗ̄ܒ ܠ

call some one happy — *jemanden glücklich nennen*;

ܛܘܒܢܐ (μακάριος) the blessed one — *der Seliger*;

ܛܝܒܘܬܐ (ṭaibūthā) goodness, bounty — *Güte*;

ܛܝܒ (ṭayyebh) v. denom. prepare — *bereiten, rüsten*

ܛܟܣܐ (ṭekhsā; τάξις) order — *Reihe*; dress — *Ausstattung*

ܛܠܐ ad. recent — *neu*; ܛܠܝܘܬܐ (ṭalyūthā) youth — *Jugend*

ܛܠܠܐ (ṭellālā) shadow — *Schatten*

ܛܠܡ (ṭᵉlam) *u.* deny — *laügnen*; ܛܠܘܡܐ (ṭālōmā) unbeliever — *Unglaübiger*

ܛܡܐܐ (ṭama) ad. impure — *unrein*

ܛܡܝܘܢ ταμιεῖον treasury — *Schatzhaus*

ܛܢܢܐ (ṭᵉnānā) zeal — *Eifer*

ܛܥܐ be unknown to (c. ܠ) — *unbekannt sein*; ܛܥܐ p. ܛܥ̈ܝܐ (ṭāʿē, ṭāʿayā) pt. act. (wandering) heretic — (*herumirrend*) *Ungläubiger*; ܛܘܥܝܝ, ܛܥܝܘܬܐ (ṭuʿyai, ṭaʿyūthā) error, idolatry — *Irrtum*, *Götzendienst*; a. lead astray — *in die Irre führen*

ܛܥܢ (ṭᵉʿen) carry — *tragen*

ܛܪܘܢܐ (ṭerōnā) τύραννος

ܛܫܐ ܛܫܝܬܐ (ṭāšīthā) hiding-place — *Schlupfwinkel*

ܝ

ܝܐܐ (ya'ē; pt. act.) ad. becoming — *passend*

ܝܐܒ ܝܐܝܒܐ (ja'ībhā) ad. craving — *begehrend*; etp. desire, crave — *wünschen, begehren*

ܝܕ, ܐܝܕܐ (yadh, 'īdhā) hand — *Hand*; ܐ' ܕܡܠܟܐ royal bounty — *königliche Freigiebigkeit*; ܒܝܕ con. through, by means of — *durch, wegen*; ܒܝܕ ܕ because — *da*; ܒܐܝܕܝ (bīdhai) through — *durch*

ܝܕܐ a. confess — *bekennen*; ܡܘܕܝܢܘܬܐ (maudyānūthā) confession of faith — *Glaubensbekenntniss*; ܫܘܕܝܐ (šūdhāyā) promise — *Versprechen*

ܝܕܥ ܝܕܥܬܐ (īdhaʿtā) knowledge, discernment — *Wissen, Einsicht*; ܝܕܝܥܐ (īdhīʿā) ad. well-known, evident — *wohlbekannt, selbstverständlich*; et. be known — *bekannt sein*; a. make known — *kund thun*; ešt. know, recognize — *wissen, erkennen*

ܝܗܒ imp. ܢܬܠ (nettel) give, put, produce, permit — *geben, setzen, hervorbringen, erlauben*; ܝ' ܐܝܕܐ

lend a hand — *aushelfen;* ܛܘܒܐ ܝ' call one happy — *einen glücklich nennen;* ܩܝܡܐ ܝ' make a covenant — *einen Bund machen;* ܢܦܫܐ ܝ' expose one's self — *sich aussetzen;* ܪܓܬܐ ܝ' grant a wish — *einem Wunsche nachkommen;* ܪܡܙܐ ܝ' give a sign, command — *andeuten, befehlen;* ܫܠܡܐ ܝ' greet — *grüssen;* ܡܘܗܒܬܐ (mauhabhthā) gift — *Gabe;* et. give over, grant — *übergeben, bewilligen*

ܝܘܠܝܢܘܣ, ܝܘܠܝܢܣ, ܐܘܠܝܢܘܣ Julian

ܝܘܡܐ, ܝܘܡ day — *Tag;* ܝܘܡܢ (= ܗܢܐ ܝܘܡܐ) to-day — *Heute;* ܟܠܗܘܢ ܝܘ̈ܡܬܐ for all time — *ewiglich;* ܟܠܝܘܡ daily — *täglich;* ܝܘܡ ܡܢ ܝܘܡ from day to day — *von Tag zu Tag*

ܝܙܒ ša. save — *retten;* ešt. pass.

ܝܠܕ ܝܠܕܐ child — *Kind;* ܡܘܠܕܐ (maulādhā) birth — *Geburt*

ܝܠܦ, ܐܝܠܦ (īleph) c. acc. aut. ܒ learn, know — *lernen, wissen;* ܝܘܠܦܢܐ, ܡܠܦܢܘܬܐ (yulpānā, malpānūthā) teaching — *Lehre*

ܝܡܐ ܡܘܡܬܐ (maumāthā) oath — *Eid*

ܝܡܝܢܐ (yamīnā) right-hand — *die rechte Hand*; s. v. ܝܗܒ

ܝܣܦ a. add. — *hinzufügen*; ܐܘܣܦ ܥܠ add to — *hinzufügen*; eta. be gathered — *gesammelt werden, hinzukommen*

ܝܥܢ etp. desire — *begehren*

ܝܥܪܐ (yaʿrā) weed — *Dorngestrüpp*

ܝܨܦ (īṣeph) c. ܕ have a care for, experience — *sorgen für, erfahren*; ܝܨܝܦܘܬܐ (yaṣīphūthā), ܨܦܬܐ (ṣephthā) care — *Sorgsamkeit*

ܝܩܕ ܝܩܕܢܐ (yaḳdānā) n. burning—*Brand*; a. burn (act.) — *verbrennen* (act.)

ܝܩܪ (īḳar) be heavy, important — *schwer, wichtig sein*; ܐܝܩܪܐ (īḳārā) glory — *Ehre*; ܝܘܩܪܐ (yuḳrā) weight — *Gewicht*; ܝܩܝܪܐ (yaḳḳīrā) ad. precious, honourable — *wertvoll, ehrwürdig*; ܝܩܝܪܘܬܐ (yaḳḳīrūthā) heavyness — *Schwere*; v. pa. honour — *ehren*

ܝܪܒ become great — *gross, viel werden*

ܝܪܚܐ, ܐܝܪܚ (īreḥ, yarḥā) month — *Monat*

ܝܪܟ (īrekh) *a.* be long — *lang sein*

ܐܘܪܚܐ (urḥā) road, way — *Weg*

ܡܬܚ *a.* extend — *ausdehnen*

ܝܬܒ (īthebh) sit — *sitzen*; ܡܘܬܒܐ (mautbā) seat — *Sitz*

ܝܬܡܐ (yāthmā) orphan — *Waise*

ܝܬܪ ܝܘܬܪܢܐ (yuthrānā) advantage — *Vorteil*; meyathrā excellence — *Vortrefflichkeit*; yattīr, ad. ܝܬܝܪ ܡܢ, ܝܬܝܪ ܡܢ ܕ more than — *mehr als*; ܕܝܬܝܪܐ ܡܢ ܟܠܗܘܢ more than all this — *mehr als dies alles*; ܠܐ ܝܬܝܪ not rather — *nicht lieber*; ܝܬܝܪ̈ܬܐ (yattīrāthā) superfluous things — *überflüssige Sachen*; ܝܬܝܪܐܝܬ (yattirā'īth) av. especially — *überhaupt*; v. etp. be increased — *vermehrt werden*

ܟ

ܟܐܒ (kebh) grieve — *leiden*; ܟܐܒܐ (kēbhā) n. pain — *Leiden*

ܟܐܢܐ (kēnā) ad. just. — *gerecht*; well-founded — *fest gegründet*; ܟܐܢܘܬܐ, ܟܢܘܬܐ righteousness — *Gerechtigkeit*; ܒܟ' av. justly, with good reason — *gerecht, mit gutem Recht*

ܟܐܦܐ (kēphā) rock, stone — *Fels, Stein*

ܟܒܫ (kebhaš) *o.* subdue — *unterwerfen*

ܟܕ (kadh) con. when, while — *als*; introduces, with or without part., a ḥāl sentence (N. § 275)

ܟܕܘ (kadū) ܡܢ ܟܕܘ now, even now — *jetzt, schon*

ܟܘܒܐ (kūbhā) thorn — *Dorn*

ܟܘܙ (kᵉwaz) be ashamed — *sich schämen*

ܟܘܪܐ (kūrā) oven, smelter — *Ofen, Schmelzer*

ܟܝܪ etp. be revered; ashamed — *geehrt sein, sich schämen*

ܟܝ (kai; enclitic) therefore — *also*

ܟܝܢܐ (kᵉyānā) nature — *Natur*

ܟܝܣܐ (kīsā) purse — *Geldbeutel*

ܟܟܪܐ (kakkᵉrā) talent — *Talent*

ܟܠܐ (kᵉlā) hinder — *hindern*

ܟܠܒܐ (kalbā) dog — *Hund*

ܟܠ, ܟܘܠ ad. all — *alle*; ܟܠܗ ܒܟܠܗ entirely — *ganz und gar*

ܟܠܝܠܐ (kᵉlīlā) crown — *Krone*

ܟܡܪ ܟܡܝܪܐ (kᵉmīrā) ad. sad — *betrübt*; ܟܘܡܪܐ (kumrā) priest — *Priester*; ܪܒ ܟܘܡܪܐ high-priest — *Oberpriester*; ܟܘܡܪܘܬܐ (kumārūthā) priesthood — *Priestertum*; ܪܒܘܬ ܟܘܡܪܘܬܐ highpriesthood — *Oberpriestertum*

ܟܢܫ (k^e^naš) *o.* be gathered, gather, collect — *sich versammeln, sammeln*; pa. gather — *sammelen*; et. pass.; ܟܢܫܐ (kenšā), ܟܢܘܫܝܐ (k^e^nušyā), ܟܢܘܫܬܐ (k^e^nuštā), gathering, assembly — *Versammlung*; ܒܝܬ ܟܢܘܫܬܐ gathering-place, place for worship — *Versammlungsort, Bethaus*

ܟܣܐ ܟܣܐ (k^e^sē), ܟܣܝܐ (kasyā) (pt. pas.) n. hidden thing — *das Verborgene*

ܟܣܣ ܡܟܣܢܘܬܐ (maksānūthā) centure, vituperation— *Tadel, Schmähung*

ܟܦܐ (kappā) palm of the hand — *Handfläche*

ܟܦܢܐ (kaphnā) ad. hungry — *hungrig*

ܟܦܪ (k^e^phar) *o.* c. ܒ deny — *verlaügnen*; ܟܦܘܪܝܐ (k^e^phuryā) infidelity — *Untreue, Unglaube*

ܟܪ av. c. ܕ where — *wo*

ܟܪܐ be sad — *trübe sein*; ܟܪܝܬ ܠܝ (keryath lī) it paines me — *es ist mir leid* (N § 254 A); pa. shorten — *ab- ver- kürzen*; ܟܪܝܘܬܐ (karyūthā) sadness — *Trauriqkeit*

ܟܪܙ et. proclaim — *Verkünden*; pa. ibid.

ܟܪܟ et. go around — *herumgehen*

ܟܘܪܣܝܐ (kursᵉyā) seat, throne — *Sitz, Thron*

ܟܪܣܛܝܢܐ (kᵉrestyānā) Christian — *Christ*; ܟܪܣܛܝܢܘܬܐ (kᵉrestyānūthā) Christianity — *Christentum*

ܟܫܦ etp. supplicate — *anflehen*

ܟܫܪ *a.* flourish — *blühen*; ܟܫܝܪܐ (kaššīrā) ad. sagacious — *scharfsinnig*; etp. be successful — *von gutem Erfolge, glücklich sein*

ܟܬܒ *o.* write — *schreiben*; et. pass.; ܟܬܒܐ (kᵉthābhā) ܟܬܝ̈ܒܬܐ (kᵉthībhāthā) letter — *Brief*; ܟܬܒܐ = ܩܕܝܫܐ 'ܟ Bible — *die Bibel*

ܟܬܦܐ (kathpa) shoulder — *Schulter*

ܟܬܪ pa. remain, continue — *bleiben, dauern*

ܟܬܫ *o.* strive — *streiten*; ܟܬܝܫܐ (kᵉthīšā) devilish one (used of Julian's soldiers) — *teuflischer (von den soldaten Julian's gebraucht)*; etp. fight — *streiten, ringen*

ܠ

ܠ sign of the objective — *objectzeichen* (N § 287); ܠܘܬ (lᵉwāth) to — *zu*; ܠܦܘܬ towards — *nach*

ܠܒܐ (lebbā) heart — *Herz* (N § 80 B I); ܠܒܝܒܐ (lᵉbhībhā) strong — *kräftig*; ܠܒܝܒܘܬܐ

(lebhībhūthā) strength — *Kraft*; pa. ܠܒܒ (labbebh) aminate — *aufmuntern*; etp. take heart — *Muth fassen*

ܠܒܛ pa. incite — *aufreizen*

ܠܒܫ (lebhaš) *a.* c. acc. be clothed — *bekleidet sein*; ܠܒܫܐ (labbāšā) ad. mailed — *gepanzert*

ܠܓܝܘܢܐ (legyōnā) legion — *Legion*

ܠܗܩ (lehak) *o.* be eager — *sich eifern*

ܠܘܐ etp. join ones self — *nachfolgen*; c. ܠ follow — *begleiten*

ܠܛ (lāṭ) (pt. pas.) ad. detested — *Verhasster*

ܠܚܡ pt. act. ܠܐܚܡ (lāhem) be proper, becoming — *passend sein*; pass. ܠܚܝܡ threaten, be indignant — *drohen, aufgebracht sein*

ܠܚܫ (lehaš) *o.* mutter incantations, murmur — *bezaubern, zuflüstern*

ܠܛܫ (letaš) *o.* sharpen (sword) — (*Schwert*) *schärfen*

ܠܝܬ (lait) is not — *ist nicht*

ܠܡ (lam) forsooth, namely — *nämlich* (N § 155 C)

ܠܡܕ ܬܠܡܝܕܐ (talmīdhā) disciple — *Jünger*; ܬܘܠܡܕܐ (tulmādhā) discipleship — *Jüngerschaft*

ܠܚܟ lick up (blood) — *(Blut) auflecken*

ܠܟܝܫܝܐ (lekīšāyā) ad. late, last one — *spät, letzter*

ܡ

ܡܐ rel. pro. ܡܐ ܕ when, whensoever — *wann, wenn* (N § 258); ܟܡܐ how many! — *wie viele!*; ܕܠܡܐ (dalmā) lest, that not — *dass nicht etwa* (N § 373)

ܡܐܐ 100

ܡܐܢܬ ܠܗ ܡܐܢ (menath leh) he was weary — *er wurde überdrüssig* (N § 254); ܡܐܢܝܘܬܐ (ma'īnūthā) sloth — *Faulheit*

ܡܐܢܐ (mānā) vestment — *Gewand*

ܡܕܡ (meddem) a thing, anything — *etwas*; ܡܕܡ ܕ that which — *das was*; ܟܠ ܡܕܡ everything — *alles*; ܕܡܕܡ ܡܕܡ of something, some — *gewisse* (N § 219)

ܡܘܣܝܩܝܪܘܬܐ (musīḳārūthā i. e. μουσικά) music — *Musik*

ܡܚܐ strike — *schlagen*; ܡܚܘܬܐ meḥōthā blow — *Schlag*

ܡܚܝܪܘܬܐ ܡܚܝܪ (maḥḥīrūthā) geometry — *Geometrie*

ܡܚܪ (meḥār) to-morrow — *Morgen*

ܡܛܠ (meṭṭul) because of, concerning — *wegen*

ܡܛܐ arrive — *ankommen*

ܡܝ̈ܐ (mayā) water — *Wasser*

ܡܝܠܐ (mīlā i. e. μίλιον) mile — *Meile*

ܡܝܬ *u.* die — *sterben*; ܕܠܐ ܡܐܬ (dela māʾeth) ad. immortal — *unsterblich*; ܡܝܬܐ (mithā) dead person — *Todter*; ܦܠܚ̈ܝ ܡܝܬܐ idolaters — *Götzendiener*

ܡܟܟ ܡܘܟܟܐ (mukkākhā) humiliation — *Demüthigung*

ܡܟܝܠ (mekkīl) therefore — *also*

ܡܠܐ be complete, fill — *vollständig sein, füllen*; ܡ' ܠܒܐ console — *trösten*; ša. perfect, carry out — *vervollkommen, ausführen*; ܡܠܐ ܙܒܢܐ (melē) for a time, temporarily — *eine zeit lang, zeitweilig*; ܡ' ܥܕܢܐ ibid.; ܡܠܘܐܐ (melōʾā) abundance — *Fülle*

ܡܠܐܟܐ (malʾākhā) angel — *Engel*

ܡܠܛ (melaṭ) *o.* be astute, shrewd — *scharf, schlau sein*

ܡܠܟ a. rule, cause to rule, take possession of — *regieren, regieren machen, in Besitz nehmen*; ܡܠܟܐ king — *König*; ܡܠܟܘܬܐ Kingdom — *Königreich*

ܡܠܠ pa. speak — *sprechen*; ܡ' ܕܝܢܐ pronounce judgement — *Urtheil aussprechen*; et. be spoken, recounted—*erzählt werden*; etp. ad. ܠܐ ܡܬܡܠܠܢܐ (la methmall^{e}lā) indescribable — *unbeschreibbar*; ܡܠܬܐ (mell^{e}thā) word, speech, account — *Wort, Rede, Erzählung*; ܡܡܠܐ (mamlā) speech — *das Reden*

ܡܢ (man) pro. rel. who — *wer*; ܡܢܘ (manū) = ܡܢ ܗܘ

ܡܢܐ (mānā) pro. rel. what, that which — *das*; pro. inter. what, why — *was, warum*; ܡܢܐ ܐܝܬ ܠܢ ܕ why should we .... — *warum sollen wir* . . .

ܡܢ (men) pr. from, because of — *von, wegen*; ܡܢ ܕ from, whenever — *von, nachdem, als*; ܡܢܗܘܢ some of them — *einige von ihnen*

ܡܢܐ ܡܢܬܐ (m^{e}nāthā) n part, portion, measure — *Teil, Mass*; ܡܢܝܢܐ (menyānā) number, era — *Zahl, Zeitrechnung*

ܡܢܥ pa. reach — *gelangen*

ܡܨܐ pt. pass. ܡܨܐ (m^{e}ṣē) be able — *im stande sein*

ܡܨܥܬܐ (m^{e}ṣa^{c}tā) middle, midst — *Mitte*

ܡܪܐ, ܡܪܝܐ (mārē, māryā) The Lord God — *Der Herr*; ܡܪ̈ܝ ܢܟܣܐ rich men — *Reiche*

10

ܡܪܚ a. be audacious — *kühn, frech sein*; ܡܪܚܘܬܐ (marraḥūthā) effrontery — *Unverfrorenheit*

ܡܪܝ (marrī) pa. c. ܒ emulate — *nacheifern*

ܡܫܚ ܡܫܘܚܬܐ (meśuḥthā) measure, span — *Mass, Spann*; ܡܫܝܚܐ (mešīḥā) Messiah — *Messias*

ܡܬܘܡ (methōm) ever — *jemals*; ܡܢ ܡܬܘܡ, ܡܡܬܘܡ (memthōm) from everlasting — *von Ewigkeit her*; ܠܐ ܡܢ ܡܬܘܡ, ܡܢ ܡܬܘܡ . . . ܠܐ never — *niemals*; ܡܡܬܘܡ . . . ܠܝܬ there is never — *niemals gibt es*

ܡܬܚ *o.* prolong — *verlängern*

ܢ

ܢܒܐ etp. profecy — *prophezeien*

ܢܓܕ et. be led — *geführt werden*

ܢܓܪ ܢܘܓܪܐ (nugrā) n. length — *Länge*; ܡܢ ܢ' since a long time — *seit langer Zeit*; ܢܓܝܪܐ (naggīrā) ad. lasting, long — *dauernd, lang*

ܢܗܪ ܢܗܝܪܐ (nahhīrā)enlightened—*erleuchtet*; ܢܗܝܪܘܬܐ (nahhīrūthā) clearness, splendor — *Klarheit, Glanz*

ܢܕ (nād) a. ܐܢܝܕ ܪܝܫ (anīdh) shake the head — *den Kopf schütteln*

ܢܚ (nāḥ) *o.* rest — *ruhen*; a. give rest — *ruhe geben*; eta. come to rest, come to an end — *sich beruhigen, zu Ende kommen*; ܢܝܚܐ (neyāḥā) rest, quiet — *Ruhe*; ܥܪܣܐ ܕܢ' bed of peace — *Bett der Ruhe*; ܢܝܚܐ (nīḥā; p. pt. pas.) ad. ܢܝ̈ܚܬܐ (nīḥāthā) courteous (words) — *höfliche (Worte)*

ܢܘܣܐ (nausā) *νάος* temple — *Tempel*

ܢܘܪܐ (nūrā) fire — *Feuer*

ܢܚܬ (neḥeth) *o.* descend, go — *herabsteigen, gehen*

ܢܚܬܐ (naḥtā) garment — *Gewand*

ܢܛܪ *a.* watch — *bewachen*; ܢܛܝܪܘܬܐ (neṭīrūthā) observance — *Bewahrung, Beobachtung*; ܡܛܪܬܐ (maṭṭartā) watch — *Bewachung*

ܢܟܐ injure — *schädigen*; a. ibid.; et. pas.

ܢܟܠܐ (nekhlā) fraud — *Betrug*; ܚܘܒܐ ܕܠܐ ܢܟܠܐ unfeigned love — *unverstellte Liebe*

ܢܟܣ ܢܟ̈ܣܐ (nekhsē) riches — *Vermögen* ܢܟܣܬܐ (nekhsethā) slaughter — *Schlachten, Gemetzel*

ܢܟܦ (nekhaph) *a. o.* be ashamed — *sich schämen*

ܢܘܟܪܝܐ (nukhrāyā) stranger — *Fremder*; v. denom. etp. renounce — *entsagen*

ܢܣܒ (nᵉsabh) *a.* take — nehmen; ܢ' ܙܟܘܬܐ obtain victory — *Sieg gewinnen*; ܢ' ܡܘܡܬܐ take an oath — *einen Eid leisten*; ܢ' ܦܘܢܣ recieve acclamations — *Zurufe entgegennehmen*; ܢ' ܫܘܠܡܐ end — *beenden*; ܢ' ܫܘܪܝܐ commence — *anfangen*

ܢܣܐ ܢܣܝܢܐ (nesyānā) proof — *Beweis*; ܢܣܝܘܢܐ (nesyōnā) trial — *Versuchung*

ܢܣܟ (nᵉsakh) *o.* infuse — *einflössen*; et. spread it's self — *sich verbreiten*

ܢܦܠ (nᵉphal) *e.* fall upon (c. ܒ), arrive — *fallen* (c. ܒ), *ankommen*

ܢܦܩ (nᵉphaḳ) *o.* issue, depart. go, come to pas. — *ausgehen*, *weggehen*, *geschehen*; a. bring forth — *hinausführen*

ܢܦܫܐ soul, self — *Seele, Selbst*; ܒܢܦܫܗ alone — *alleine*; ܡܢ ܢܦܫܗ of his own accord — *unaufgefordert*; ܚܝ̈ܐ ܕܢܦܫ̈ܬܟܘܢ your life — *dein Leben*

ܢܨܚܢܐ (neṣḥānā) triumph — *Sieg*

ܢܨܪܝܐ (nāṣrāyā; Nazarene) Christian — *Christ*

ܢܩܕܐ (naḳdā) ad. pure — *rein*

ܢܩܦ (nᵉḳeph) *a.* c. acc join — *anhängen*, *sich gesellen zu*

ܢܩܫ (nᵉḳaš) *o.* smite — *schlagen*

ܢܫܡܬܐ (n^{e}šamthā) soul, breath — *Seele, Atem*

ܣ

ܣܒܐ (sābhā) old man — *Greis*; ܣܝܒܘܬܐ (saibūthā) old age — *Greisenalter*

ܣܒܠ *o.* c. ܒ aut. acc. carry, bear — *tragen*; a. cause to carry, bear, inflict — *tragen machen, auferlegen*

ܣܒܥ be filled, satiated — *voll sein, sich sättigen*; etp. ibid.

ܣܒܪ hope, expect, imagine — *hoffen, erwarten, sich einbilden*; pa. c. acc. aut ܠ tell, announce — *mittheilen, verkünden*; et. be supposed, imagined — *vermuthet sein*; ܣܒܪܐ (sabhrā) hope — *Hoffnung*; ܡܣܒܪܢܐ (m^{e}sabb^{e}rānā) messenger — *Bote*; ܡܣܝܒܪܢܘܬܐ (m^{e}saibrānūthā) patience — *Ausdauer*

ܣܓܕ (s^{e}gedh) *o.* worship — *verehren*; et. pas; ܣܓܕܬܐ (segd^{e}thā) n. worship — *(Gottes)dienst*

ܣܓܐ ܣܓܝܐܐ, ܣܓܝܐ (saggī'a) ad. many — *viele*; ܣܘܓܐܐ (sōgā) n. multitude — *Menge*

ܣܕܩ (s^{e}dhak, s^{e}dhek) *o.* tear — *zerreissen*; et. pas.; pa. tear in pieces — *in Stücke reissen*; ܣܕܩܐ (sedhkā) n bit — *Stück*

ܣܕܪܐ (sedhrā) right order, course, row — *Ordnung, Reihe*

ܣܗܕ pa. persuade — *überzeugen*; a. ibid.; ܣܗܕܐ (sāhᵉdhā; pt. act.) n. witness, martyr — *Zeuge, Märtyrer*; ܣܗܕܘܬܐ (sāhdūthā) martyrdom — *Märtyrtum*

ܣܘܐ wish — *begehren*

ܣܐܒ. (sābh) ܡܣܝܒܐ (mᵉsayyᵉbhā; pa. pt. pas.) ad. abominable — *abscheulich*

ܣܘܚ pa. desire — *wünschen, begehren*

ܣܟ ܣܟܐ (sākhā) n. end — *Ende*; postpos. at all — *überhaupt*

ܣܘܣܝܐ (susyā) horse — *Pferd*

ܣܘܦ exhale — *ausatmen*

ܣܚܦ (sᵉḥaph) *o.* cast down — *stürzen*

ܣܚܪܬܐ (sāḥartā) palace — *Palast*

ܣܛܐ turn aside — *abbiegen*

ܣܛܢܐ (sāṭānā) Satan

ܣܡ appoint, ordain, collect, affirm — *anstellen, ordiniren, sammelen, bestätigen*; ܐܦܐ 'ܣ resign one's self, make up one's mind — *entsagen, sich entschliessen*; ܢܦܫܐ 'ܣ devote one's self — *sich ergeben*;

ܣ' ܬܢܘܝ̈ make a pact. — *Bund schliessen*; et. be placed, gather, prepare one's self — *gestellt werden, sammelen, sich vorbereiten*; ܣܝܡܬ ܒܢܝ̈ܐ (sīmath b^enayā) adoption — *Ankinden*

ܣܘܟܠܐ (sukkālā) intelligence — *Einsicht, Verstand*; ܡܣܟܠܢܐ (mask^elānā) evil-doer — *Sünder*

ܣܟܢ ܡܣܟܢܐ (meskēnā) ad. poor — *arm*

ܣܠܩ (s^eleḳ) *a.* come, arrive, ascend — *kommen, ankommen, heraufsteigen*

ܣܡܟ (s^emakh) *o.* rest, reach, approach — *ruhen, erreichen, (sich) nähern*

ܣܢܩ (s^eneḳ) need — *bedürfen*; ܣܢܝܩܐ (s^enīkā) ad. needy — *bedürftig*

ܣܥܪ *o.* visit — *besuchen*; et. be done, do, act. — *gemacht sein, thun, handeln*; ܣܘܥܪܢܐ (su^crānā) action, visit — *That, Besuch*

ܣܥܪܐ (sa^crā) hair — *Haar*

ܣܦܐ (s^ephā) n. (lip) side, edge — (*Lippe*) *Seite, Kante*; ܣܦܐ ܒܣܦܐ from one end to the other — *von einer Seite bis zu der andern*

ܣܦܩ (s^ephaḳ) *a.* be able — *vermögen, können*

ܣܦܪ pa. cut the hair — *Haare schneiden*

ܣܩܘܪܐ (sūḳōrā) enemy — *Feind*

ܣܪܚ *o.* destroy — *vernichten*; ܣܘܪܚܢܐ (surḥānā) fault, crime — *Schuld, Verbrechen*

ܣܪܩ ܣܪܝܩܐ (serīḳā) ad. empty (word) — *leeres (Wort)*; ܣܪܩܐ (serḳā) comb[instrument of torture] — *Kamm [zum Foltern gebraucht]*; — etp. be deprived of, renounce — *beraubt sein, sich entsagen*

ܣܬܪ *o.* overturn, destroy, hide — *überwerfen, zerstören, verbergen*; et. pas.

ܥ

ܥܐܕܐ (ʿēdhā) festival — *Fest*

ܥܒܕ (ʿebhadh) make, do, appoint — *machen, thun, anstellen*; ܥ' ܚܘܫܒܢܐ ܥܡ call some one to account — *einen zu Reschenschaft ziehen*; ܥ' ܟܬܒܐ write a letter — *einen Brief schreiben*; ܥ' ܦܘܩܕܢܐ publish a decree — *Gebot ausgeben*; ܥ' ܦܘܪܩܢܐ redeem — *auslösen*; ܥ' ܫܘܒܩܢܐ release — *befreien, loslassen*; ܥ' ܫܠܡܐ make peace — *Frieden schliessen*; ܥ' ܬܒܥܬܐ punish — *strafen*; ܥ' ܬܢܘܝ make a pact — *Bund schliessen*; ܥܒܝܕ

pt. pas. set, appointed — *angestellt*; ܥܒܘܕܐ (ʿābhōdhā) creator — *Schöpfer*; ܡܥܒܕܢܘܬܐ (maʿbhdānūthā) machination — *Anstiftung*

ܥܒܪ *a.* pass away — *vorbei sein*; ܗܘܐ ܕܥܒܪ the past — *Vergangenheit*; ܡܬܥܒܪܢܐ (methʿabhrānā) offender — *Missethäter*; ܡܬܥܒܪܢܘܬܐ (methʿabhrānūthā) offence — *Missethat*

ܥܓܠ ܒܥܓܠ (baʿgal) av. quickly — *schnell*

ܥܕ (ʿadh) while — *während*; ܥܕ ܠܐ before — *bevor, ehe*; ܥܕܡܐ ܠ unto, up to, as far as, until — *bis, so weit als*; ܥܕܟܝܠ (ʿedhakkēl) until, as yet — *bis auf, bisher*

ܥܕܐ c. ܥܠ come upon — *stossen auf*

ܥܕܪ succour — *helfen, beistehen*; ܥܘܕܪܢܐ (ʿudhrānā) n. help — *Hilfe*; ܡܥܕܪܢܐ (meʿadderānā) helper — *Helfer*; ܡܥܕܪܢܝܐ (meʿadderānāyā) ad. helpful — *nützlich*

ܥܝܕܐ (ʿeyādhā) custom — *Gewohnheit*

ܥܘܙܐ (ʿuzzā) strength — *Kraft*

ܥܘܟ et. be hindered — *gehindert sein*; ܡܥܘܟܢܐ (meʿawwekhānā) one that hinders — *einer der hindert*

11

ܥܘܠܐ (ʿaulā) wickedness — *Frevel*

ܥܩ (ʿāḳ) ܥܩܬ ܠܝ (ʿāḳath lī) it grieves me — *es schmerzt mich* (N § 254 A)

ܥܘܪ etp. be blinded — *geblendet sein*

ܥܪ (ʿār) be awake, keep watch over — *wach sein, bewachen*; eta. wake up — *aufwachen*

ܥܡܐ et. become extinct — *erloschen werden*

ܥܝܢܐ (ʿainā) eye — *Auge*; ܥܝܢ ܒܓܠܐ (ʿēn bagelā) av. openly — *offen*

ܥܠ pr. upon, unto, concerning, because, (c. ܕ) in regard to, against — *auf, zu, wegen, (auch c.* ܕ), *betreffs, gegen*

ܡܢ ܠܥܠ (men leʿel) above — *oben*

ܥܠ (ʿal) *o.* come, enter (c. ܒ), fall upon (c. ܥܠ) — *kommen, eintreten* (c. ܒ), *überfallen* (c. ܥܠ); ܥܠ ܒܩܝܡܐ make a covenant — *Bund schliessen*; ܡܥܠܬܐ (maʿalthā) n. coming — *Ankunft*; ܥܠܝܐ (ʿelāyā) ad. upper — *obere*; n. The Most High — *Der Höchste*; ܡܥܠܝܐ (meʿalyā) ad. elevated — *hoch*; ܥܠܬܐ (ʿellethā) cause — *Ursache*; ܒܥܠܬܟܘܢ (beʿellathkhōn) because of you — *deinetwegen*; ܡܛܠ ܥܠܠܬܐ ܕ because of — *wegen*

ܥܠܬܐ (ʿelāthā) p. ܥܠܘܬܐ (ʿelawāthā) heathen altar — *heidnischer Altar*

ܥܠܐ a. c. ܒ sin — *sündigen*; etp. be removed — *entfernt sein*; eš. be arrogant — *anmassend sein*

ܥܠܡ, ܥܠܡܐ (ʿālām, ʿālmā) n. world — *Welt*; ܨܦܬܗ ܕܥܠܡܐ worldly cares — *weltliche Sorgen*; ܕܡܢ ܥܠܡ from eternity — *von Ewigkeit her*; ܠܥܠܡ for ever — *ewiglich*; ܕܠܥܠܡ ad. everlasting — *immerwährend*

ܥܠܝܡܐ (ʿelaimā) n. youth — *Jüngling*; denom pa. give back youth — *verjüngen*

ܥܡ pr. with, in comparison with — *mit, im Vergleich mit*

ܥܡܡܐ people — *Leute*

ܥܡܠ *a.* work — *arbeiten*; ܥܡܠܐ work — *Arbeit*

ܥܡܪ ܥܘܡܪܐ (ʿumrā) dwelling-place — *Wohnung*; ܡܥܡܪܐ (maʿmārā) ibid.; ܥܡܘܪܐ (ʿāmōrā) inhabitant — *Bewohner*

ܥܢܐ (ʿānā) sheep, flock — *Lamm, Heerde*

ܥܢܢܬܐ (ʿannāthā) perverse — *verstockt*

ܥܢܕ *a.* die, remain far from (c. ܡܢ) — *sterben,*

fernbleiben von (c. ܡܢ); ܥܘܢܕܢܐ ܡܢ ܥܠܡܐ (ʿundānā) death — *Tod*

ܥܣܪܐ 10; ܥܣܪܝܢ 20

ܥܩܒܐ (ʿeḳbhā) heel — *Ferse*; ܒܥܩܒܐ ܕ (in the footsteps of) after — (*in den Fusstapfen von*) *nach*; s. v. ܐܬܪ; ܥܩܒܬܐ (ʿeḳbethā) footstep — *Fusstapfen*

ܥܘܩܣܐ (ʿuḳṣā) sting — *Stich*

ܥܩܪ *o.* uproot — *ausreissen, entwurzeln*

ܥܘܪܠܐ (ʿurlā) ad. uncircumcised — *unbeschnitten*

ܥܪܣܐ (ʿarsā) bed, couch — *Bett*

ܥܪܨ (ʿeraṣ) *a.* c. ܥܠ happen to — *geschehen*

ܥܪܩ (ʿeraḳ) *o.* flee — *fliehen*

ܥܫܢ (ʿešen) *a.* become strong — *stark werden*; ܥܘܫܢܐ (ʿušnā) strength — *Stärke*; pa. continue — *fortdauern, bleiben*

ܥܬܝܕܐ (ʿethīdhā) pt. pas. prepared — *bereit*; ܥܬܝ̈ܕܬܐ things to come — *zukünftige Sachen*

ܥܬܝܩܐ (ʿattīḳā) ad. old things — *das alte* (II Cor. V, 17); ܥܬܝܩܘܬܐ (ʿattīḳūthā) old age — *Greisenalter*

ܦ

ܦܐܝ be beautiful, becoming — *schön sein, geziemen*

ܦܐܪܐ (pērā) fruit — *Frucht*

ܦܓܥ c. ܒ happen upon, befall — *begegnen, widerfahren*

ܦܓܪܐ (pagrā) body — *Leib*

ܦܓ (pāg) a. temper — *mildern, mässigen*

ܦܘܡܐ mouth — *Mund*

ܦܘܢܣ φωνάς acclamations — *Beifälle, Zurufe*

ܦܫ (pāsh) c. ܡܢ desist — *abstehen*

ܦܚܡܐ (peḥmā) copy — *Abschrift*; ܒܪ ܦܚܡܗ his like, equal — *seinesgleichen*

ܦܝܠܘܣܘܦܘܬܐ φιλοσοφία

ܦܝܣܐ (πεῖσαι) denom, a. be persuaded, persuade — *übereded sein, übereden*

ܦܠܓ (p^{e}lag) *o.* ܐܝܩܪܐ 'ܦ give honour — *Ehre erweisen*

ܦܠܚ *o. u.* work, cultivate, worship — *arbeiten, bebauen, anbeten*; ܦܘܠܚܢܐ (pulḥānā) work, service — *Arbeit, Dienst*; ܦܠܚܐ (pallāḥā) workman, farmer — *Arbeiter, Ackersmann*

ܦܠܛ et. escape — *entrinnen*

ܦܠܥܐ (pelʿā) opportunity — *Gelegenheit*

ܦܢܐ [turn]; ܦܢܝܐ (pānyā) n. eventide — *Abend*; ܦܘܢܝܐ (pūnāyā) return — *Zurückker*; et. turn to (c. ܠܘܬ) — *sich zuwenden* (c. ܠܘܬ); repay — *zurückerstatten*; pa. = ܦܢܐ ܦܬܓܡܐ answer — *antworten*

ܦܣ (pas) a. grant permission — *erlauben*

ܦܣܥ overstep — *überschreiten*

ܦܣܩ *o* ܦ'ܣܩܝܗ determine — *entscheiden*; ܦܣܝܩܬܐ n. p. ܒܦܣܝܩܬܐ (baphesīḳāthā) av. briefly — *mit wenig Worten*; ܦܘܣܩܢܐ (pusḳānā) decree — *Gebot*

ܦܥܠܐ (pāʿlā) n. worker — *Arbeiter*

ܦܦܝܣ Papias

ܦܩܕ *o*. command — *befehlen*; et. pas.; ܦܩܘܕܐ (pāḳōdhā) commander), head — (*Befehlshaber*), *Spitze*

ܦܩܚ pt. ܦܩܚܐ (pāḳeḥā) be seemly, becoming — *schicklich sein*

ܦܩܪ become insane — *wahnsinnig werden*; ܦܩܪܐ (paḳrā) ad. mad. — *wahnsinnig, wüthend*

ܦܪܓ a. pt. ܡܦܪܓ (mapbreg) ad. beautiful, splendid — *schön*

ܦܪܗܣܝܐ παρρησία; 'ܒ av. openly — *öffentlich*

ܦܪܘܬܠܝܣ nomen prop.

ܦܪܢܣ (parnes) arrange, administer, dispense — *ordnen, verwalten, verteilen*

ܦܪܣ. (p^{e}ras) *o.* extend — *ausbreiten*; et. be diffused — *ausgebreitet sein*; ܦܘܪܣܐ πόρος purpose, trick — *Plan, List*; ܐܝܟ ܕܠܦܘܪܣܐ ܕ for the purpose of — *damit*

ܦܪܥ *o.* 2 acc. visit upon, repay — *vergelten* ܦܘܪܥܢܐ (purʿānā) recompense — *Vergeltung*

ܦܪܨܘܦܐ (parṣōpā) πρόσωπον face — *Gesicht*

ܦܪܩ *o.* abandon — *verlassen*

ܦܪܫ *o.* understand — *verstehen*

ܦܫܛ ܦܫܝܛܐ (p^{e}šīṭā) ad. simple-minded — *Schlicht*

ܦܫܟ ܦܘܫܟܐ (puššākhā) uncertainty — *Unsicherheit*

ܦܫܪ et. be dissolved — *geschmolzen sein*

ܦܬܓܡܐ (pethgāmā) word — *Wort*

ܦܬܚ *a.* open, commence — *öffnen, anfangen*; et. pas.; ܦܘܬܚܐ (puttāḥā) n. opening — *Öffnung*

ܦܬܟܪܐ (p^{e}thakhrā) idol — *Götzenbild*; ܒܝܬ ܦܬܟܪܐ heathen Temple — *Tempel*

ܨ

ܨܒܐ v. wish, desire — *wollen*; c. ܒ delight in — *wohlgefallen haben an*; ܨܒܘܬܐ (ṣ^{e}bhūthā) thing, p. (ṣebhwāthā) affairs, contents — *Sache, p. Geschäfte, Inhalt*; ܨܒܝܢܐ (ṣebhyānā) wish, desire, intention, will — *Wunsch, Wille, Absicht*

ܨܗܐ be thirsty — *dursten*

ܨܘܪܐ (ṣaurā) neck — *Halz*

ܨܚܐ ܨܘܚܝܬܐ (ṣōḥīthā) scorn — *Schmähung*

ܨܝܕ (ṣēdh) pr. at, towards — *bei, zu*

ܨܠܝܒܐ (ṣ^{e}lībhā) cross — *Kreuz*

ܨܠܚ a. prosper — *gedeihen*

ܨܠܐ pa. pray — *beten*

ܨܠܥ pa. rend, tear — *zerreissen*

ܨܢܥܬܐ (ṣenʿ^{e}thā) snare, guile — *Falle, List*

ܨܥܪܐ (ṣaʿrā) contempt — *Schmähung*; ܡܨܥܪܢܘܬܐ (m^{e}ṣaʿrānūthā) ibid.

ܨܦܪܐ (ṣaphrā) early morning — *Frühmorgen*

ܩ

ܩܒܠ pa. recieve — *empfangen*; eš. arrive — *ankommen*; ܠܘܩܒܠ, ܠܩܘܒܠܐ (luḳbhal, l^{e}ḳubhlā) pr. towards, against — *nach, gegen*

ܩܒܪ *o.* bury — *begraben*

ܩܢܐ pa. acquire — *erwerben*

ܩܕܡ pa. proceed — *vorangehen*; ܩܕܡ (ḳedhām) pr. before — *vor*; ܡܢ ܩܕܡ ibid.; ܠܘܩܕܡ (luḳdam) ad. first — *erste*; ܕܡܢ ܩܕܡ (demen ḳedhām) ad. first, previous — *erste, vorhergehend*; ܩܕܡܝܐ (ḳadhmāyā) ad. av. first — *erster, erst*; ܩܕܡܐܝܬ (ḳadhmā'īth) av. firstly — *zuerst*

ܩܕܫ ܩܘܕܫܐ (ḳudhšā) sanctuary — *Heiligtum*; ܩܕܝܫܐ (ḳaddīšā) ad. holy — *heilig*

ܩܘܐ pa. ܩܘܝ ܒܚܝܐ remain alive — *am Leben bleiben*

ܩܠܐ (ḳālā) voice — *Stimme*

ܩܘܣܛܢܛܝܢܘܣ Constantine

ܩܡ (ḳām) stand — *stehen*; a. carry out, place — *durchführen, setzen*; etp. be carried out — *ausgeführt werden*; ܩܝܡܐ (ḳeyāmā) resurrection, covenant, clergy, members of the church — *Auferstehung, Bund, Klerus, Kirchenmitglieder*; ܩܝܘܡܐ (ḳāyōmā) overseer — *Vorsteher*; ܡܩܝܡܢܐ (meḳīmānā) sustainer — *Erhalter*

ܩܛܠ *o.* kill — *töten*; et. pas.; ܩܛܠܐ (ḳeṭlā) slaughter — *Mord, Gemetzel*

ܩܛܥ ܩܘܛܥ ܪܥܝܢܐ (ḳūṭaʿ reʿyānā) dejection of mind — *Niederschlagenheit*; etp. c. ܠ despair — *verzweifeln*

12

ܩܛܝܪܐ (ḳᵉṭīrā) necessity — *Notwendigkeit*; ܡܢ ܩܛܝܪ forcibly — *gewaltsam* (N § 155 B)

ܩܠܐ etp. be vexed — *erzürnen*

ܩܠܝܠ (ḳallīl) ad. av. little — *Wenig*: ܕܠܝܠܐ ܩܠܝܠ (dallīlā ḳallīl) a very few — *sehr wenig*

ܩܠܣ pa. praise — *preisen*; et. pas.; ܩܘܠܣܐ (ḳullāsā) praise — *Preis*

ܩܠܪ̈ܘܣ κλῆρος

ܩܢܐ possessed of, acquire — *erwerben, besitzen*; ܩܢܝܢܐ (ḳenyānā) possession — *Besitz*

ܩܢܛܐ (ḳenṭā) fear — *Furcht*

ܩܢܘܡܐ (ḳᵉnōmā) person, self — *Person, Selbst*

ܩܥܐ cry out — *schreien, rufen*

ܩܦܠܐ (ḳāpēlā) κάπηλος huckster — *Höcker*

ܩܨܐ (ḳeṣā) n. end — *Ende*

ܩܨܡܐ (ḳeṣmā) divination — *Wahrsagung*

ܩܩܢܐ (ḳeḳnā) plow — *Pflug*

ܩܪܐ summon, invite, read — *rufen, einladen, lesen*; et. be read — *gelesen werden*; be obstinate — *hartnäckig sein*; ܩܪܝܢܐ (ḳeryānā) reading — *Lesen*

ܩܪܒ (ḳᵉrebh) *o.* draw near, be near — *sich nähern*; pa.

bring near — *nahe bringen*; ܩܘܪܒܐ (ḳurbā) n. proximity — *Nähe*; ܩ' ܕ almost — *beinahe*
ܩܪܝܒܐ (ḳerībhā) n. relative — *Verwandter*;
ܩܘܪܒܢܐ (ḳurbānā) offering — *Opfer*

ܩܪܝܪܐ (karrīrā) ad. cool — *kühl*

ܩܪܣܐ (ḳērsā) καιρός; ܐܪܥ ܩ' v. fight — *kämpfen*

ܩܘܫܬܐ (ḳuštā) truth—*Wahrheit*; p. ܕܠܩܘܫܬܝܢ (dalekuštīn) ad. av. true, in truth — *wahr, führwahr* (N § 155 A)

ܩܫܝܐ (ḳašyā) ad. tough — *hart, zähe*

ܪ

ܪܒܐ (rabbā) great one, chief — *Haupt*; ܪܒ ܚܝܠܐ general — *Heerführer*; p. ܪܘܪܒܢܐ leaders — *Führer* (N § 146)

ܪܒܐ v. increase — *zunehmen*

ܪܓ (rag) ܪܓܬܐ (reggethā) wish — *Begierde*; etp. desire — *begehren*

ܪܓܙ (regez) *a.* be incensed — *zürnen*; ܪܘܓܙܐ, ܪܓܝܙܘܬܐ (rugzā, regīzūthā) anger — *Zorn*

ܪܓܡ *o.* stone — *steinigen*

ܪܓܫ (regaš) *a.* c. ܒ get wind of — *ausfindig machen, bemerken*

ܪܕܐ walk, be well-versed — *wandern, bewandert sein*

ܪܕܝܘܬܐ (radhyūthā) mode of life — *Lebensart*

ܡܪܕܘܬܐ (mardūthā) discipline — *Zucht*

ܪܕܦ ܪܕܘܦܐ (rādhōphā) persecutor — *Verfolger*; ܪܕܘܦܝܐ (redhuphyā) persecution — *Verfolgung*

ܪܗܒ etp. be afraid — *erschrecken* (intr.); ܣܪܗܒ (sarhebh) hasten — *eilen*; ܡܣܪܗܒܐܝܬ (mesarhebhā'īth) hastily — *eilig*

ܪܗܘܡܐ Rome; ܪܗܘܡܝܐ (Romāyā) Roman — *Römer*

ܪܗܛܐ (rehṭā) course, life — *Lauf, Leben*

ܪܒ (rābh) c. ܥܠ clamour — *lärmen*; a. storm (in words) — *toben (mit Worte)*

ܪܘܙ (rewaz) *a.* c. ܒ rejoice — *frohlocken*

ܪܘܚܐ (rūhā) wind — *Wind*; ܪܘܚܢܐ (rūḥānā), ܪܘܚܢܝܐ (rūḥānāyā) ad. spiritual — *geistich*

ܪܘܡ (rūm) be lifted up (voice) — *erhaben sein (vom Stimme), laut sein*; a. lift up (voice, sword), remove — *erheben (Stimme, Schwerdt), entfernen*; eta. be haughty — *stolz sein*: ܪܡܐ (rāmā) ad. high, towering, uplifted (voice) — *hoch, laut (Stimme)*

ܪܐܙܐ (rāzā) secret — *Geheimniss*; ܒܐܪܙ (ba'rāz) av. secretly — *heimlich*

ܪܚܡ (reḥem) *a.* love — *lieben*; ܪ̈ܚܡܐ (rāḥmē)

mercy — *Gnade*; ܡܪܚܡܢܘܬܐ (m^{e}raḥ-mānūthā) beneficence — *Wohlthätigkeit*

ܪܫܐ, ܪܝܫܐ (rēšā) head, beginning — *Kopf, Anfang*; ܡܢ ܪܝܫ; ܡܕܪܝܫ (medd^{e}rēš) av. from the beginning, afresh — *vom Anfang an, vom Neuen*;

ܪܝܫܢܐ (rīšānā) n. chief — *Haupt*

ܪܟܒ (r^{e}khebh) *a.* ride (ܪ' ܣܘܣܝܐ) — *reiten*

ܪܟܢ (r^{e}khen) *a.* decline (day, shadow) — *neigen (Tag, Schatten)*; a. incline, bend (head) — *beugen (Kopf)*

ܪܡܐ. pt. pas. ܪܡܐ ܗܘܐ he was cast — *er war hingeworfen*; a. cast — *werfen*; et. devote, submit one's self, yield — *weihen, sich unterwerfen, hergeben*; a. c. ܥܠ put a duty upon — *einem etwas auferlegen*

ܪܡܙܐ (remzā) hint, sign — *Wink, Zeichen*

ܪܢܝܐ (renyā) concern — *Gedanke, Besorgniss*

ܪܥ (raʿ) *o.* break, appease — *brechen, besänftigen*

ܪܥܐ (pt. act.) n. ܪܥܝܐ (rāʿyā) shepherd — *Hirt*; ܡܪܥܝܬܐ (marʿīthā) flock — *Herde*; ܪܥܝܢܐ (reʿyānā) thought, mind—*Gedanke, Anschauung*; etp. intend, be reconciled — *gedenken, versöhnt werden*

ܪܦܐ ܪܦܝܘܬܐ (raphyūthā) negligence — *Nachlässigkeit*

a. ܐܝܕܐ ܐܪܦܝ loose hold, let go — *loss-lassen, fahrenlassen*; etp. relax — *locker werden* c. ܡܢ fall away from — *abfallen*

ܪܦܣ (rephas) *o.* stamp with the foot — *stampfen*

ܪܘܙ pa. make sport — *sich belustigen*

ܪܫܡ (rešam) *o.* inscribe, write down — *aufzeichnen*

ܪܫܝܥܐ (raššīʿā) ad. wicked — *frevelhaft*

ܪܬܐ a. admonish — *ermahnen*

ܫ

ܫܐܕܐ (šēdhā) sprite — *Demon*

ܫܐܠ (šel) ask — *fragen*; pa. ibid.; etp. c. ܡܢ abstain from, deny — *sich enthalten von; läugnen*

ܫܒܬܐ, ܫܒܐ (šabbā), (šabbethā) p. ܫܒ̈ܐ (šabbē) sabbath s. v. ܒܝܬ

ܫܒܚ ܫܒܝܚܐ (šebhīḥā) ad. renowned, praiseworthy, glorious — *berühmt, preiswürdig, rühmlich*; pa. praise — *preisen*

ܫܒܥܐ 7; ܫܒܥܝܢ 70

ܫܒܩ (šebhaḳ) *o.* leave, discard — *lassen, verwerfen*; ܫܘܒܩܢܐ (šubhḳānā) release, condonation — *Entlassung, Vergebung*

ܫܓܫ et. be perturbed — *beunruhigt sein*

ܫܕܐ throw, drive — *werfen, hinaustreiben*; c. ܡܢ throw off — *abwerfen*; ܩܠܐ 'ܫ roar — *brüllen*

ܫܕܪ pa. send — *schicken*; etp. pas.; ܡܫܕܪܢܐ (m^e^šadd^e^rānā) sender — *Sender*

ܫܗܐ pa. extinguish — *löschen*

ܫܘܐ v. merit — *würdig sein*

ܫܘܩܐ (šuḳā) street, market place — *Strasse, Marktplatz*

ܫܘܚܛܐ (šuḥḥāṭā) perversity — *Eigensinn*

ܫܘܡܬܐ (šumtā) scar — *Narbe*

ܫܚܝܡܐ (š^e^ḥīmā) ad. simple — *einfach*; ܫܚܝܡܐܝܬ av. simply — *einfach*

ܫܚܪ etp. remain — *bleiben*

ܫܟܚ ܐܫܟܚ (eškaḥ) find, be able — *finden, können*; et. be found, happen — *gefunden werden, geschehen*; ܫܟܚܬܐ (š^e^khāḥtā) notion — *Idee*; 'ܡܫ ܕܐܠܗܐ godliness — *Frömmigkeit*

ܫܝܢܐ (šainā) peace — *Friede*; ܡܫܝܢܢܐ (m^e^šainānā) pacifier — *Friedenstifter*

ܫܟܢ (š^e^khen) *a.* dwell — *wohnen*; pa. bestow — *schenken*; a.

cause to dwell, populate, bestow — *wohnen machen, bevölkern, schenken*

ܫܠܚ *o* send — *schicken*; et. pas. — ܫܠܝܚܐ (š^{e}līḥā) apostle — *Apostel*

ܫܠܛ (š^{e}laṭ) *a*. c. ܒ rule over — *beherrschen*; etp. c. ܥܠ ibid.; ܫܘܠܛܢܐ (šulṭānā) dominion — *Herrschaft*

ܫܠܐ c. ܡܢ desist — *ablassen*; ܫܠܝܐ (šelyā) n. quiet — *Ruhe*; ܗ̄ܘܐ ܫܠܝܐ desist — *ablassen*; ܡܢ ܫܠܝܐ av. suddenly — *plötzlich*

ܫܠܡ (š^{e}lem) *a*. be completed, consent — *vollendet sein, sich fügen*; ܫܠܡܐ (š^{e}lāmā) peace — *Friede*; ܫܘܠܡܐ (šullāmā) end — *Ende*; ܫܠܡܘܬܐ (šalmūthā) agreement — *Übereinkunft, Einwilligung*; pa. confirm, fulfill — *bestätigen, erfüllen*; a. hand down — *überliefern*

ܫܡܐ name — *Name* (N § 146); ܡܫܡܗܐ (m^{e}šamhā) ad. renowned — *berühmt*

ܫܡܛ (š^{e}maṭ) *o*. draw (the sword) — *(das Schwert) ziehen*

ܫܡܝܐ (š^{e}mayā) the heavens, heaven — *Himmel*

ܫܡܥ c. ܒ vel ܥܠ hear of — *von einer sache hören*; a. relate, notify — *erzählen, benachrichtigen*; et. was heard, be obedient to (c. ܠ) — *gehört werden, gehorsam*

sein (c. ܠ); ܡܫܡܥܢܘܬܐ (mašmʿanūthā) obedience — *Gehorsam*

ܫܡܫ pa. serve — *dienen*; ܡܫܡܫܢܐ (mešammešānā) deacon, heathen priest — *Diacon, heidnischer Priester*; ܬܫܡܫܬܐ (tešmeštā) sacred vessels — *heilige Gefässe*

ܫܢܬܐ (šenthā) n. sleep — *Schlaf*

ܫܢܬܐ (šattā) p. ܫܢ̈ܝܐ (šenayā) year — *jahr*

ܫܢܐ ܫܢܝܐ (šānyā pt.) ad. crazy — *wahnsinnig*; etp. become crazed — *wahnsinnig werden*; ܫܢܝܘܬܐ (šenāyūthā)aberration, madness—*Verirrung, Wahnsinn*

ܫܢܕܐ (šendhā) torture — *Marter*

ܫܥܬܐ (šāʿthā) hour — *Stunde*; ܟܠܫܥ (kulšāʿ) every hour, always — *jede Stunde, immer*; ܗܫܐ (hāšā = ܗܐ ܫܥܬܐ) now — *jetzt*; ܡܢ ܗܫܐ from now on — *von nun an*

ܫܥܘܬܐ (šeʿūthā) wax — *Wachs*

ܫܥܐ ܬܫܥܝܬܐ (tashʿīthā) story — *Erzählung*

ܫܦܝܐ (šaphyā) ad. pure — *rein*

ܫܦܥ ܫܦܝܥܐ (šephīʿā) liberal — *reichlich*; a. show abundantly, pour forth — *reichlich zeigen, ausgiessen*; etp. be freely given — *reichlich gegeben sein*

13

ܫܦܪ c. ܠ be pleasing — *gefallen*; ܫܘܦܪܐ (šuphrā) glory — *Ruhm, Preis*; ܫܦܝܪ (šappīr) ad. well — *wohl, gehörig*

ܫܩܠ *o.* lift up, proceed, take, win — *aufnehmen, fortschreiten, nehmen, gewinnen*; ܫܘܠܡܐ 'ܫ end — *endigen*; ܫܩܝܠ ܠܢ (pt. pas.) has been brought, told, to us — *ist uns gebracht, erzählt worden*; eta be proud — *hochmütig sein*; ܡܫܩܠܬܐ (mᵉšaḳḳalthā) ad. arrogant — *anmassend*

ܫܪܐ loosen, let free, dismiss — *looslassen, befreien, weckschicken*; pa. commence — *anfangen*; et. be set free — *frei gelassen werden*; ܫܘܪܝܐ (šūrāyā) beginning — *Anfang*; ܡܫܪܝܬܐ (mašrīthā) camp — *Lager*

ܫܪܝܢܐ (šeryānā) cuirass — *Panzer*

ܫܪܟܐ (šarkā) n. the rest — *Rest*

ܫܪ ܫܪܪܐ (šᵉrārā) truth, rectitude — *Wahrheit, Redlichkeit*; ܫܪܝܪ (šarrīr) ad. true, assured — *wahr, gewiss*; ܠܐ ܫܪܝܪܐ ܗܘܬ ܠܗ he was not certain — *es war ihm nicht sicher*; etp. be confirmed, assured — *befestigt, bestätigt sein*

ܫܬܐ ܫܬܬܥܣܪ 16; ܫܬܝܢ 60; ܫܬܡܐܐ 600

ܫܬܐܣܬܐ (šethestha) foundation — *Fundament*

ܫܬܩ (šᵉtheḳ) *o.* be silent — *schweigen*

ܬ

ܬܐܒܝܠ ܬܒܝܠ (tēbhīl תֵּבֵל) world — *Erde, Welt*

ܬܒܥ *a. o.* seek, demand — *suchen, fordern*; ܬܒܥܬܐ (t^ebhaᶜthā) punishment — *Strafe*

ܬܒܪ *a. o.* break, destroy, conquer — *zerbrechen, vernichten, besiegen*

ܬܐܓܐ (tāgā) crown — *Krone*

ܬܓܪ s. v. ܐܓܪ

ܬܘܗܝܐ (tuhhāyā) ܕܠܐ ܬ' without delay — *ohne Zögerung, sofort*

ܬܗܪ wonder — *sich wundern*; c. ܒ marvel at — *sich staunen über*; a. cause wonder, please — *in Staunen setzen, gefallen*

ܬܘܐ feel compunction — *bereuen*

ܬܒ (tābh) a. c. ܦܬܓܡܐ answer — *antworten*; ܬܘܒ (tūbh) again, further — *wieder, ferner*

ܬܘܗ (t^ewah) v. wonder — *sich erstaunen*

ܬܘܪ (t^ewar) be astonished — *sich wundern*; ܬܘܝܪܘܬܐ (tawwīrūthā) stupor — *Betaübung*

ܬܚܘܡܐ (t^eḥōmā) ܬܚܘܡܗ ܕܥܕܬܐ the precincts of the Church, the Church and its surroundings — *Bereich der Kirche, die Kirche und seine Umgebungen*

ܬܚܝܬ (t^{e}ḥēth) pr. beneath — *unter*; v. denom. ܬܚܬܝ humiliate — *demüthigen*

ܬܟܠ pt. pas. trust, be certain — *vertrauen, gewiss sein*

ܬܠܐ etp. c. ܒ seize — *greifen*

ܬܠܥ etp. be torn — *zerissen sein*

ܬܠܬܝܢ 30; ܬܠܬܡܐܐ 300

ܬܡܗ (t^{e}mah) v. wonder — *sich wundern*; ܬܡܝܗܐ (t^{e}mīhā) ad. wonderful — *wunderbar*; ܬܡܝ̈ܗܬܐ (t^{e}mīhāthā) wonderful things — *wunderbare Sachen*

ܬܡܢ (tammān) ad. there — *dort*

ܬܩܢ (t^{e}ḳen) *a.* be restored, put in good order — *wiederhergestellt sein*; et. ibid.

ܬܩܦ (t^{e}ḳeph) *a.* be strong — *stark sein*; ܬܘܩܦܐ (tuḳpā) power, vigour — *Stärke, Macht*

ܬܪܝܢ ܬܪܬܝܢ 2; ܕܬܪܬܝܢ in the second place — *zweitens*

ܬܢܘܝ (tanwai) pact — *Bedingung*

ܬܪܥܐ (tar^{c}ā) door, gate — *Thür, Pforte*

ܬܪܨ (t^{e}raṣ) *o.* make a bee line for — *direkt hingehen*; ܬܪܝܨܐ (t^{e}rīṣā) ad. straight — *gerade*; ܗܝܡܢܘܬܐ ܬܪܝܨܬܐ orthodoxy — *Rechtglaübigkeit*

ܬܫܥܝܢ 90; ܬܫܥܡܐܐ 900

Zeitfracht Medien GmbH
Ferdinand-Jühlke-Straße 7
99095 Erfurt, Deutschland
produktsicherheit@kolibri360.de